TRAPSTAR

Book One

BLAKE KARRINGTON

MARVA FARRIS

Chapter One

LUCKY ME

A shiny 2012 White Range Rover Sport came to a smooth stop perfectly in the parking space. The vehicle was one of the trappings of success; a symbol of luxury. Behind the wheel sat a young gorgeous African American female named Brianna Campbell. Through her Dolce & Gabbana shades, she glanced down at the platinum Rolex watch on her wrist. It read one o'clock. She was right on time for her hair appointment.

As soon as she entered the hair salon, Brianna noticed that all eyes were on her. Still, she remained cool behind her dark tinted shades. It would take more than a few envious eyes to unnerve her. Although Hera by Him was an upscale hair salon, it wasn't free from the catty gossip that plagued every hood shop. As soon as Brianna strolled past, almost immediately the whispers and speculation began.

With of all the high priced designer accessories and clothes Brianna wore, the majority of the women assumed that she was some ball players' girlfriend or wife. The large six carat diamond ring did little to dispel those rumors. There was no denying that she was well kept. Her outfit and designer bag caused some insecure women to fall back into obscurity when they saw her. They knew all her accessories were real, while most of theirs were bootleg; cheap knock offs.

Usually all clients were required to wait in the sitting area until they were called by their stylist, but not Brianna. She strolled right pass the receptionist, heading straight to the back. The receptionist merely glanced at Brianna, but she didn't attempt to stop her. She recognized that Brianna was a regular. But besides that Brianna had a swagger about her that suggested that she wasn't to be messed with.

Her stylist seemed to light up when she saw Brianna coming towards her. It wasn't because she was happy to see her or that liked doing her hair either. Brianna paid well; it was as simple as that. The stylist knew that she wouldn't have to do another head that day. Once Brianna was done tipping her, she was going to be straight.

"Hey Bri." The stylist happily said. "I can set my watch to you girl, you always on time. I wish all my clients were like you."

Lauren was one of the few people Brianna knew she could never allow to get a peek into her life. She had witnessed first hand the way Lauren spoke about her other clients and their personal business. So no matter how friendly her stylist was to her, Brianna was always the same; nonchalant. She always gave her the cold shoulder, shutting down any attempts at them becoming too friendly. All the idle chitchat that went on between stylist and client didn't exist when she took her seat in the stylist's chair. Brianna guarded her privacy like a celebrity. Brianna simply smiled in response to the comment.

After taking off her shades and placing them inside her bag, she handed her personal items to her stylist, who put the bag under the counter.

In the mirror Lauren smiled as she examined different parts of Brianna's weave. She could feel Brianna watching her. She went from the front to the back inspecting her hair. When

2

she reached the back she grimaced slightly. Thankfully Brianna didn't catch it.

A large scar on the back of Brianna's head had caused this reaction. Brianna's scar betrayed her pampered appearance. What in the world was a woman of Brianna's stature doing with such an ungodly scar was beyond Lauren. As a matter of fact it was the subject of debate whenever Brianna left the salon. To her credit the stylist never asked any questions, and Brianna never offered an explanation.

Lauren could tell she had been through some shit, but what she didn't know. She would have loved to find out.

Quickly pushing those thoughts out of her mind, she went to work. Meanwhile, Brianna casually looked around. While Lauren moved about in the booth Brianna took notice of her attire. She was dressed in a black t-shirt and black jeans. Brianna looked down to see what she had on her feet and instantly she got pissed.

"Fuckin' Jordan's!' She cursed to herself.

Those sneakers would be forever stoned in Brianna's memory. It didn't matter if they were worn by a male or female, she hated them. As she closed her eyes Brianna's mind began to trace back to the moment that she had not been able to erase. Suddenly her thoughts began to run wild.

THE HALOGEN HEADLIGHTS shone brightly from the four door European sedan, illuminating the entire garage. With a touch of a button, the garage door quickly closed. Calmly the two occupants of the car made their exit. Tre led the way inside the house. After placing his key into the lock, he entered the house and punched in his security code, deactivating the alarm. His girlfriend Brianna followed closely behind. The couple had just come home from a busy night on the town. Brianna loved going out, she like being in the spot light. But

Tre was the total opposite. In Tre's line of work it was better to be talked about rather than seen. The streets of Charlotte, NC were like a jungle, filled with both predators and prey. But by no means was Tre anybody's prey. On the contrary, he was just as dangerous as they came. But, to meet Tre for the first time one would never know. He had a very laid back disposition, and would rarely be seen in jeans or any of the latest urban wear. He had learned along time ago, that the quieter you were the easier it was to move.

Inside the luxurious confines of his townhouse, Tre breathed a sigh of relief. .

"Umm, that steak was good as shit!" he suddenly announced. "I'm full like a motherfucker."

He flopped down on the couch, kicked back and relaxed. Reaching for the television remote, he turned on the 63 inch plasma TV. Quickly he became captivated by the new Rick Ross video that was airing on BET. He was feeling extremely sluggish. The big meal he had eaten had begun to take effect.

Meanwhile, in the hallway Brianna began to get comfortable herself. She slipped off her high heel shoes, loosened the buttons on her blouse and made her way toward the living room.

"Hold on Big Poppa." Brianna said. "Don't go to sleep on me yet. I got something way better than that steak!"

To Tre that could only mean one thing, some good head. Like the old saying went, 'The way to a man's heart may have been through a man's stomach'. But for Tre it was threw his dick. He went fool over some good head. And nobody did it better, than Brianna.

Immediately, Brianna got down on her knees and went to work. Quickly she unzipped Tre's pants, reaching inside she gripped his dick, pulled it out and took it into her mouth. Brianna's mouth was warm and wet. She began licking and sucking on the head of his dick. She worked her way down until every inch was in her mouth. Moving faster and faster until she felt his dick grow harder and harder. Brianna used just the right amount of spit and suction. Tre drop his head back and sighed.

Again and again, he thrust his hips to meet her hungry mouth. With his eyes closed he enjoyed the moment.

"Damn baby Suck dat dick!" He cursed. "Do dat shit."

Tre's cursing didn't even bother Brianna. She was with whatever it took to get him off. She knew if she didn't, there were plenty other hoes, out in the streets, who would jump at the opportunity. She felt if he was going to stray, it wasn't going to be because of anything she did or didn't do.

"Cum in my mouth daddy!" Brianna demanded.

The commandment drove Tre crazy. He quickly obliged. A hot jolt of semen shot from his balls to the head of his dick, into Brianna's warm and waiting mouth. As soon as it came out, she gobbled it up and swallowed it down. When she had drained every last drop of his love juice, Brianna continued to suck on his dick. Unable to take any more, Tre tried to pry her lips off.

"Alright, God damn!" He exclaimed. "Brianna, that's enough."

From the floor, Brianna glanced up at her man. A sinister smile spread across her face. She knew it was a job well done.

Getting up off her knees, Brianna proudly stood above her man.

"Nigga, git up." She joked. "It wasn't all like that."

Tre lay on the couch in the fetal position, trying to regain the little bit of energy, he had just lost.

"Shiiittttt!!!" Was all he managed to say.

Brianna insisted. "C'mon, Tre stop playin'. Git up and come wit me upstairs to the shower. Let's get ready for bed.
"

"You go 'head." He told her. "I'll be up there in a minute."

"Promise."

"Promise!" He replied. "I'll be right up there as soon as I get myself together."

"Alright, hurry up!" She demanded. "We ain't finished yet. We got one more round to go."

Reluctantly, Brianna walked away to prepare for their next sexual romp to take place in the shower. She hurried along in anticipation of what was to come. She had just turned the corner, taking only a few steps out of the living room when suddenly two masked gunmen appeared.

With the barrel of a semi-automatic weapon pointed directly at her forehead, Brianna didn't utter a word. Instinctively, she backed up as the gunmen moved silently toward her. The TV successfully drowned out any noise they made.

Quickly, the two masked men pushed Brianna into the living room, brandishing their weapons on Tre. Caught completely off guard, Tre just stared in disbelief, wondering how in the hell had these two niggas gotten into his house without setting off the alarm system.

The larger one barked. "Nigga, make a move and I'm gonna let you feel this heat."

Immediately, the other man snatched up Brianna. Everything appeared to be moving in slow motion to her.

Brianna was violently shoved onto the couch. With a gun pointed in her face, she couldn't do anything but stare. The gunman and his weapon were oblivious to her, for whatever reason her eyes were locked on the man's hand. All she could see was the word 'Smalls' in cursive writing tattooed on the bottom of his hand.

"Bitch, don't look at me!" The gunman growled. "Turn ya fuckin head'!"

Either Brianna moved too slowly or it wasn't fast enough. Whatever the case was the gunman, viciously slapped her. Brianna head recoiled violently from the blow. She fell back onto the couch with the taste of blood quickly filling her mouth.

"Ok, you know what it is. Just give us what we came for."
The larger one demanded. "Now where the stash at?"

"Nigger ain't nuttin' here!" Tre snapped. "I don't eat where I shit."

Unfortunately, the gunmen didn't buy a word he was saying. Without warning the large man, began to pistol whipped Tre. He was thrown to the floor where he was kicked and beaten some more. Blood began to flow freely from a gash in his head.

"Nigga, you think this a muthafuckin' game huh?" He yelled. "Now, I'ma ask you one more time. Where is it at?"

By now Brianna was in a state of shock. She didn't understand why Tre didn't just give them what they wanted so they could leave. She thought it was just that simple.

"Look, I already told you niggas. Ain't nuttin' here." He muttered through a pair of swollen lips.

A third man entered the room. With a nod of his head, he motion to the one who had Brianna, to lift her up. His partner reacted by reaching down, grabbing a handful of Brianna's hair, and snatching her up off the couch. He placed one arm around her neck, the other hand clutched the gun that was pressed to her temple.

"Nigga, you better tell us what we wanna hear and fast." The other gunman spat. "The next muthafuckin' lie you tell, this bitch is dead! Now, where's the stash at?"

Though he was more than a little woozy, Tre was still defiant. He glared angrily at his two assailants. An evil thought ran through his mind, 'If I can get to one of my guns. I'm going to kill these motherfuckers.

Amongst all the commotion, the shouting, the threats and the violence, the videos were still playing on the television, a tomb like silence suddenly enveloped the room. The threat of death hung in the air.

For what seemed like an eternity no one said a word. Brianna eyes suddenly locked with Tre's. They seemed to sing a sad song. They pleaded with Tre to give up the goods. Still he stood his ground, refusing to say a thing.

Seeing this Brianna knew she would be forced to take matters into her own hands. She felt it was the only way to remedy the situation, since Tre wasn't talking.

"It's upstairs in the bedroom." She blurted out. "The money is upstairs in the bedroom in a suitcase."

'Damn!' Tre cursed to himself. He shot her an ice cold stare.

Tre would have rather her give up the location of the dope than the money. Money was too hard to come by. Now he had to take some more pen chances to recoup his cash. While if he was robbed of some drugs, he could go to his drug connection and get more on consignment.

The gunmen released his grip on Brianna, who stood there holding her throat. Trying to recover from the choke hold she had been in. Taking two steps away from her, suddenly the gunmen turned back around and viciously struck her with the butt of his gun. Caught off guard, Brianna went crashing face first to the floor. She was knocked unconscious by a blow to her temple.

The other two gunmen laughed heartily, signaling their approval.

"Damn, you knocked that bitch out cold." one commented. "Now go upstairs and get the money."

Doing as he was told, the second gunman fled the living room, and went to retrieve the money.

The larger gunman announced, "Nigga, ya girl smarter than you. You lucky she told us when she did. I thought we was gonna have to kill her ass, just for you to talk. Just for that we gonna let ya'll live."

Tre didn't believe a word the man had said. But he wasn't really focused on him anyway. It was the third man who didn't speak a word that concerned him the most. It was obvious he was the one running things.

Before Tre could give it any real thought or get himself together to mount an attack, he heard the other gunman come running down the stairs. It was then that he realized that he may have blown his only chance of survival.

"You got it?"

"Yeah, I got it! It was right where she said it was." He laughed.

Tre watched as the other gunman entered the room and gave the bag to third man. At that point he sensed that something was up, though no more words were exchanged between the men. It was as if he knew what was about to happen.

With two large caliber firearms trained on him, Tre watched as the men inched closer and closer, until they were within pointblank range. Something came over him that he hadn't felt in years, it was fear. Though he had personally sent countless individuals to the afterlife, now that it was his turn, suddenly he realized he didn't want to go. He wasn't ready to leave this earth, not at the ripe old age of twenty five years old. He had so much more living to do and things to see. He couldn't believe it was ending like this.

Tre wasn't a chump, but he knew he didn't want to die.

With the finality of the situation close at hand, Tre finally backed down off his defiant stance, his lumped shoulders now suggested he had gone into submission. A pitiful look appeared on his face, one that invited any act of divine intervention. Tre's look invited any act of mercy, so that his life and that of his girlfriend might be spared.

The gunmen shot him a cold look of indifference, one that seemed to suggest that they would not deviate from their plan. Their hard core looks condemn him and his girlfriend to their fate, which was death.

Suddenly without warning, Tre lunged for one of gunman's firearms. If he was going to die, he wasn't going down without a fight. Too bad he wasn't quite fast enough to execute his plans. Gunshots exploded through the room. Six bullets found their mark. When the smoke cleared Tre was slumped on the floor, dead.

"Now, finish the bitch! And let's get the fuck outta here!" The first gunman screamed.

Standing above Brianna, he had a chance to see her innocent beauty. Even though she was covered in blood, her face was captivating. He closed his eyes and fired two shots, one missed badly and other drew blood, but it only grazed her head.

Brianna lay motionless on the floor. The gunman thought he had successfully executed her.

Long after the gunmen were gone, Brianna continued to lie on the floor, playing dead. She wanted to be sure no one was going to double back, to finish the job. As she looked around, she saw Tre's lifeless body lying in a pool of blood. For a long time she lay there thinking about Tre. It was heartbreaking to see him like that. Though he was certainly no angel Tre didn't deserve to go out like that.

THAT NIGHT AT THE HOSPITAL, a weeping Brianna sat for hours answering every question that the police threw at her.

"Ma'am, could you tell us why someone would want to hurt you and your fiancé?" The older white cop asked.

"You said robbery earlier, but it didn't seem like they took anything of value." The other cop spoke.

Brianna knew she couldn't tell them exactly what happen, there were still drugs at the house. And she didn't know how much. She cleverly sprinkled lies in with the truth. She knew she needed to get home and get the dope out the house. Or she would not only be losing Tre, but possibly her freedom. The FEDS didn't care who did the time as long as someone did it.

When the police left, Brianna checked herself out the

hospital. She couldn't bring herself to stay in the house that night. So she checked herself into a hotel. While she lay on the bed, she looked up at the ceiling. She wished she had a family to lean on, but she knew hers was not an option. Her family life had never been what a little girl deserved. Especially one who had both parents. This was now her second time, being alone, and having no one to turn too. As she fell asleep she reflected on her childhood.

Chapter Two

HARD KNOCK LIFE

Brianna Campbell always has been a dreamer. She loved fairytales with happy endings. Ever since she was a child she loved to pretend. Brianna was a latchkey child, raised on unhealthy amount of television and movies. She idolized black actors and actresses, to the point that she could quote and re-enact some of the most famous parts, line for line. Her room was like a sanctuary.

Life in the Campbell household wasn't the same for Brianna as it was for her two other younger siblings, Jonathan and Charrise. Almost from day one, she sensed that there was preferential treatment shown to her younger sister and brother. It wasn't until she was around nine years old that she found out the reason why. At Brianna's ninth birthday party things finally came to a head. And the truth was revealed.

"HOW OLD ARE YOU NOW? How old are you now..." The partygoers chanted.

In the darkened kitchen, the nine candles on the store bought chocolate birthday cake, illuminated the room.

Brianna hovered dangerously close to the cake, staring into the candles as if she were hypnotized. She enjoyed being the birthday girl, the center of attention. Sadly, she knew that her moment in the spotlight would fade quickly. Still she lived in the moment. Like any good actress, Brianna played her part well. Outwardly, she grinned ear to ear at her adoring guests. Inwardly, she hurt badly.

As she scanned the room, looking at each familiar face, one was noticeably absent, her Dad's. For some strange reason, he never participated in anything dealing with her. By now, it was routine, still it didn't hurt any less. She always noticed that he constantly shied away from her. Often Brianna wondered what she had done to deserve this.

"Brianna blow out the candles baby and make a wish!" Her mother urged her.

"Ok."

Inhaling deeply, Brianna summoned all the air her tiny lungs could hold and blew out the candles. Momentarily the kitchen went pitch black; the partygoers began to cheer loudly. When the lights came back on tears could be seen running down Brianna's rosy cheeks. Despite how it appeared, these weren't tears of joy.

"Oh, look at her she's so happy she's crying." One parent suggested.

But Lorraine Campbell knew otherwise. If there was one thing she knew, it was her children. She knew their temperaments and tendencies. And this was completely out of character for Brianna. She wasn't emotional at all. Lorraine sensed that something was very wrong.

Gently her mother took Brianna by the hand, and whisked her away from her guests. She led her straight to the bathroom.

"What's wrong with you?" She asked. "What are you crying for?"

Though she tried her best to keep her composure, Brianna

couldn't. Her tears continued to flow freely, now her body was racked by long hard sobs. Young Brianna merely stood in front of her mother unsure of what to say or do.

Her mother replied, "Don't just stand there looking all sorry. Say something! How else will I know what's the matter with you?"

After shedding a few more tears, finally Brianna mustered up the courage to tell her mother exactly what was bothering her.

"Where my Daddy?" She began. "How come he never comes to my birthday parties, huh? He always here for Jonathan's and Charrise's."

Her question caught Lorraine off guard. She hadn't expected this at all. But in the back of her mind she knew this day would come.

It was Lorraine's turn to be dumbfounded. She didn't know where to begin. But she knew that she had some explaining to do and fast.

"Brianna," She began. "The man you know as your father is not your father. He's your sister's father and your brother's father. But he's not your father."

Brianna exclaimed, "Huh? I don't believe you. You're a liar mommy!"

Brianna began to have a temper tantrum, she flailed her arms wildly at her mother. Dozens of light blows rained down on her mother's mid-section.

Unable to control her daughter's violent outburst, Lorraine reached down and viciously slapped Brianna across her face. This seemed to bring her back to reality. Pain exploded across her cheek. She stopped her antics and clutched the side of her face.

Through clenched teeth her mother spoke, "Listen Miss and listen good. Herman is not your father. He is nothing to you. You and him have no blood relations. And that's that!"

Though Brianna couldn't comprehend everything her

mother had said. But she understood enough. She got the message loud and clear. From that moment on Brianna was forced to grow up fast. She didn't like her mother's explanation but she had to accept it. For now it would be the only one she would get. It would be years before she knew the whole story.

Her mother and her stepfather, Herman, were high school sweethearts. When Herman went off to the army, following graduation, Lorraine had gotten weak and had a one night stand. Brianna was the product of that affair. But since Herman came home on leave around the same time she had gotten pregnant, and they too had intercourse, she chose to blame Herman for the paternity of the child.

The other guy was a local thug, who had nothing going for himself, other than being handsome. On the other hand, Herman had plans and goals that he was working towards. He was merely using the military as a stepping stone.

Some years later, unable to deal with her guilty conscious any more, Lorraine admitted her mistake to her husband. She received a severe beating as a reward for her honesty. Still Herman couldn't bring himself to leave his family. Against his better judgment, he stayed. Herman too was the product of a broken home. To his credit, he wouldn't let one act of infidelity break up his happy home.

Even though Herman had forgiven Lorraine, he could never forget. Everyday he was reminded of her infidelity when he looked at Brianna. He grew to despise her. As the years went on, he became abusive towards her. Not physically but mentally. Sometimes that was just as bad. His harsh words stung Brianna.

'You ain't cute. I don't know what you stay in the mirror for all day?' he commented. 'You ain't shit! And you ain't never gonna be shit! Your sorry ass daddy wasn't shit! Look he don't even care about you!'

Brianna was an A/B student, passing her classes with

flying colors. One marking period she hadn't done so well. She received two C's. And her stepfather seized the opportunity to criticize and degrade her.

He spat, "Look at this shit here! You're so stupid. How you gonna fail gym?"

Her stepfather had degraded her time and time again, right in front of her mother. When she looked to her mother for support, she got none. Not once did her mother come to her aid and defend her. She did what she always did; Lorraine pretended not to hear it. Little by little, this caused Brianna to have animosity and resentment towards her mother.

Since Herman had money, he got away with murder around the house. Lorraine tolerated his cruelty towards her daughter because he was a good provider. A local businessman, Herman owned a string of soul food restaurants throughout Charlotte. She was just as much a dependent as her children were on her husband. She dared not voice her opinion in any way shape or form. She did her best to avoid the wrath of Herman. Lorraine knew when Herman got mad he got even financially by withholding funds.

Even though her younger sister and brother weren't nearly as bright as her, they always seemed to get the benefit of the doubt. When they failed a class, they failed because the teacher didn't like them. When she failed it was because she was just too dumb.

Over the course of time, her stepfather succeeded in slowly stripping her of her self-esteem. Brianna's grades began to suffer. She became a prisoner in her own home. She chose only to leave her room for one of three things, to go to school, use the bathroom and to eat. She avoided her stepfather as if he had an infectious disease.

Lorraine felt her daughter's pain, but truthfully she was powerless to stop the abuse. With her husband's blessing she decided to seek out Brianna's father. Secretly Herman had hoped that the girl's father would take her to live with him.

One day, Lorraine walked into her daughter's room and surprised Brianna. She told her to hurry up and get dressed, that her father was coming over to meet her. Instantly Brianna's face lit up, she felt reinvigorated as if a burden had been lifted off her.

Brianna got dressed in her best clothes, she raced downstairs and sat on the front porch eagerly awaiting her dad. Each passing car carried Brianna's hopes for a better life. And with each passing car, she was devastated more and more. Hours went by, with no sign of her father. Still Brianna didn't move from that spot, she never gave of hope. She sat there until the sun began to set. Finally, her mother had seen enough, she summoned Brianna inside the house. Lorraine was just as disappointed and heartbroken as she.

"C'mon in the house, Bri. That nigga ain't coming!" She cursed. "Don't worry about it baby. He missed out on a good thing not meeting you. It's gonna be alright! I promise, it's gonna be alright!"

Her mother's reassuring words did nothing for her. If anything they contributed to her ill feelings. Silently she cursed the day she was born. All she ever wanted was a mother and a father. Was that too much to ask for?

Tears began to well up in Brianna eyes. Suddenly she took off like a rocket, racing up the stairs. When she reached the second floor, she spotted her stepfather exiting the bathroom. He had a shit eating grin pasted to his face as their eyes met.

Brianna continued to run, racing past him to her room. She slammed the door and locked it. Throwing herself on the bed, she cried herself to sleep.

All throughout her formative years, Brianna had to endure this treatment. She became a stranger in her own house to everyone but her younger sister Charrise. The two had to keep their friendship a secret. She was the only person in her household that showed her genuine kindness. Maybe she wasn't going to be shit after all.

THE WESTSIDE OF CHARLOTTE had long been a breeding ground for top flight hustlers and ruthless killers. That was where Treshaun Ellis, aka Tre, hailed from; LaSalle Street, the Betty's Ford section to be specific. Almost from the time he was born, his life revolved around the streets. Both of Tre's parents were hustlers. His father Wally was a low level drug dealer. And his mother Marva was a booster, who stole clothes, for the entire neighborhood to buy. At one point or another, one or both of Tre's parents were in prison serving time for their parts in some botched crime. Subsequently, young Tre was raised by his maternal grandmother, on and off.

A day young Tre would never forget was the day his parents were killed. Fresh out of prison, Marva was looking extremely beautiful; Wally concocted a scheme to make money. He sent her out into the nightclubs of Charlotte, with form fitting clothes, in search of hustlers. Marva would then bed the hustlers, sexing them on a regular basis. As she did so, she gathered information on them. Like where they lived, what kind of guns they had or how much money was in the house. Their plan met success the first few times. Wally and his friend successfully robbed a few weak hustlers. With each conquest, the couple grew greedy for more.

Word had quickly spread on the street about the duo. They had gone to the well one too many times. After robbing one big time hustler, a hit was placed on them. Shortly after the order was given, Wally and Marva were found dead in the trunk of a car. They were both shot execution style in the back of the head. There were no witnesses to the crime and police never captured the triggerman.

Death seemed to further complicate Tre's already nomadic life, leaving a void in it. The murder of his parent's left him feeling more vulnerable and more broken than ever. He grew up thinking life wasn't fair.

From that point on, young Tre knew that life had no happy endings in store for him. He figured that his life could be only what he made of it. With both sources of income gone, Tre slowly began to gravitate towards the street. His neighborhood was filled with negativity and eventually he felt obliged to engage in it.

Originally, Tre got into the game to provide for, not only himself, but his grandmother too. He saw her struggling for the basic necessities, food, clothing and shelter. He didn't want to become another added burden upon her.

Around that time, Tre began to have a strange fascination with streets. With negativity all around him, he began to look up to the local drug dealers. They had money, the finer things in life, jewelry, pretty women and expensive rides that they flaunted on a regular basis. There was one drug dealer in particular that Tre idolized, named Petey. Tre worshipped the ground Petey walked on. After all, Petey was a ghetto superstar.

Petey believed that life came down to dollars and cents; either you had money or you didn't. It was as simple as that. He was prepared to hustle to get it.

Only five years older than Tre, Petey carried himself like a much older hustler. Just like Tre, he came from a family of hustlers; his daddy ran a pool-hall speakeasy and his older brother was a dope boy. Petey's entire family was involved in the game, in one way or another. It was almost expected that he would follow suit. And when he did no one even raised an eyebrow.

Out of all the kids in the neighborhood, Petey took a liking to Tre. This was because Tre would do anything he asked of him. Petey was no fool, he knew a soldier when he saw one. For the disenfranchised black youths like Tre, he was a godsend.

Petey was a smooth dude, he was a lover and fighter, a gangster and a gentleman all rolled up into one. He was everything Tre wanted to be. But most of all he was a character who had game for days. There was always a reason behind everything he did.

"Nigga, you got some money in ya pockets?" He would always ask.

"No." Tre replied. "I ain't got nothin'."

"Here's a lil sumthin' sumthin'!"

From a thick wad of bills, Petey peeled off a crisp twenty dollar bill and hand it to Tre. His eyes lit up, like it was Christmas. There had never been a time in his life that anyone just given him something without expecting something in return. That random act kindness went a long way with Tre. It instilled a sense of loyalty in him for Petey. From that day forward, no one could ever say anything bad about Petey; not around him. Talking bad about Petey was like talking bad about his late mother.

Petey became like a big brother or mentor of sorts. Soon Tre became his sidekick, his 'little partner' as Petey referred to him as. Before Tre knew it he was running errands for him. Half of the time he didn't know the danger he was in. Tre became a drug courier, helping to distribute Petey's poison all over town.

For his efforts Tre received little or no money. Petey gave him just enough so that Tre would always need him. When it came to the drug game Petey passed along whatever wisdom he could impart and Tre soaked it all up like a sponge.

Like so many other young black males in the neighborhood, Tre viewed the drug game as his ticket out of the ghetto. He immersed himself in the murky, shark infested waters. Sink or swim, he was all in.

"Look nigga, you gotta always make sure you got a least three broads on ya team. The first broad she ain't a hood chick, should either work or go to school getting' an education. She wants somethin' out of life. That's your future wife. The second broad is a soldier; she holds the money and the work at her crib. She gotta be trustworthy. That's your vice president; if somethin should happen to you then she can take over. And the third broad she just a hood rat, somebody from the neighborhood you can keep the product at her house if needed. Even turn her house into a dope house if necessary." Petey explained.

These were rules to the game that Tre would always remember. He knew that they were tried and true because he watched Petey implement them everyday. As time went on Tre became more valuable to Petey. He carefully played his position while patiently waiting his turn.

Sadly just like everyone else Tre ever loved, Petey died tragically, but not by an assassin's bullet. The word on the street was that Petey was poisoned. Although there was no medical evidence to substantiate such a claim, Tre had his suspicions. Women were Petey's Achilles heel; he was never good with them. So Tre trying to find the killer to avenge him was like finding a needle in a haystack. Petey had too many.

Tre had been the one to find Petey and rush him to the hospital. He was there at the hospital, along with a few members of Petey's family, when in the predawn stillness, he took his last labored breath.

The mournful sounds of his mother's cries, along with the steady bleeps and hisses of the life support machines, could be heard throughout the room. It shattered the eerie silence of death. Unable to bear it, Tre exited the room to mourn his mentor's passing.

Petey's death would prove to be bittersweet to Tre. He was thrust into the role of the man, in the hood. His only wish was that Petey was still alive to see it.

As a result of Petey's passing a bloody drug war ensued.

The death toll seemed to mount daily. Dealers were scrambling to takeover the turf that once belonged to him. Quickly Tre had organized a team that took on all comers. When the smoke cleared Tre had emerged victorious. But he would forever be a marked man.

Just like Petey had controlled the neighborhood drug traffic for years, so did Tre. He ruled the neighborhood drug game with an iron fist. His reign of terror enabled him to hold it down for several years by instilling the fear of God in his rivals. Murder was his favorite weapon of intimidation. Whenever there was a problem, he made examples.

SEEKING to getaway from the house, on the way home from school Brianna made a short diversion to Eastland Mall. It was a trip that would forever change her life.

For hours, Brianna window shopped at every store from Foot Locker, the Downtown locker room to Marshall's. She dreamed of owning all the name brands that she saw in those stores. Her stepfather treated her like a step-child in every sense of the word. When it came time to buy her school clothes, he made sure she got little or no money. Most times, Brianna's mother would have to take money from the other children's shopping allowance.

Standing outside of one store, Brianna starred at the mannequin that was modeling a cute pink Rocawear tennis skirt with a matching shirt. Unbeknownst to her, a pair of guys had slid up behind and began admiring her body. Even though she was shabbily dressed there was no denying her body or her beauty.

The moment Tre laid eyes on her, it was clear that he was attracted to her. He was smart enough to look pass her less than up to par apparel. He saw what her step father would never see; potential. He was awestruck by her beauty. Tre knew he had to have her.

"You'd look good in that." He said with a playful smirk. "Girl I can see you now."

Brianna simply smiled; she didn't know what else to do. Even at seventeen, she wasn't used to boys approaching her.

"You want that?" He asked. "Say the word and it's yours."

Brianna shot the handsome stranger a perplexed look that seemed to say, 'You can't be serious.' Still she felt she had nothing to lose and everything to gain.

"Well, if you wanna buy it for me, I'll take it." She said meekly.

He replied, "C'mon beautiful let's go get it."

This chance meeting turned into a makeshift shopping spree. Brianna entered the store with intentions on only getting one outfit. Instead she came out with an entire wardrobe.

After they finish shopping Tre took her out to eat. It was there that they learned more about each other. Instantly Tre knew that this was one of the chicks that he needed in his life. He felt that Brianna was wifey material, just like that his mentor Petey had described. She was green to the streets so he knew that he could easy manipulate and mold her. Her good looks were just icing on the cake.

On that day, fate had finally smiled on Brianna. It had brought someone in her life that could not only care for her but support her emotionally. She didn't have that type of support at home. Tre would become her mother and her father. Someone she could turn to in times of need.

AFTER A YEAR OF COURTSHIP, when Brianna graduated from high school, she moved in with Tre. When she left home, her mother didn't so much as protest her move. Things had gone from bad to worse. Her husband and her daughter couldn't stand the sight of each other. Besides, she had two other children to worry about. Silently she wished her daughter well.

Chapter Three

WHERE'S THE LOVE?

Death never comes at a good time. For Brianna its timing couldn't have been worse. Her boyfriend had left so many loose ends behind it was ridiculous. Most people don't plan for their death, especially not drug dealers. When one lives on the outside of the law, they tend to live in the moment, so there are no wills. There is no paper trail to trace money owed out to them or their hidden assets.

Since Tre was in the upper echelon of drug dealing, this only compounded the problem. After his passing, everyone immediately assumed that Brianna was sitting on some dough, especially Tre's relatives. Their inquires about his finances and assets lead her to believe that they were more interested in that than finding the people who were responsible for his death.

Fortunately, Brianna was able to collect enough money off the streets to give Tre a proper burial. She managed to have a little left over for the bare necessities. After that she was hard pressed to crap up another dime.

Some dealers who had owed Tre large amounts of money for drug packages given to them on consignment, balked at paying giving Brianna the runaround, claiming they had already paid or just they didn't answer their phones. However bad they felt about his death, they weren't about to take a step backwards. This was the ultimate come up, one that had put many of them on their feet. They were not about to blow that once in a lifetime opportunity by showing some sense of moral responsibility. Any thoughts that they had of doing a good deed, like handing over the money, were an afterthought.

Brianna was left to bear the brunt of this burden. Right after the funeral everyone started showing their true colors. It was clear to her that all the love she had enjoyed while Tre was alive was long gone. Everybody was in flip mode.

For days after the funeral, Brianna did a combination of two things. She moped and mourned around the house that she had once shared with her boyfriend, unsure of exactly what was in store for her in the future.

One thing about being alone in the house that Brianna enjoyed was that it was alive with memories of Tre. All around the house there were various photos of him, riding in his big boy truck, the Infiniti QX56 SUV with '24 inch chrome rims. Some photos showed the couple spending a night out on the town. Others showed him posing for pictures at the club with his boys.

Tons of images seemed to flash through her head, as she relived the lasting memories that they shared. One image that would be forever be etched in her memory banks was Tre lying on the floor next to her, dead.

According to the Coroner's report, the official cause of Tre's death was a gunshot wound to the back of the head. But Brianna knew the real cause of death. His tragic death had been caused by his life in the streets.

She stared at the pictures for hours on end. They became therapeutic to her, a way for Brianna to cope with Tre's death. They reminded her of a time in the not so distant past, when it was all good. It made her realize how quickly sugar can turn to shit. One could work a lifetime to acquire material things, or a good relationship for that matter, and lose it in the blink of an eye.

Still it was her present situation that disturbed her, life without her man. She wondered what she was going to do without him.

There was no doubt that Tre was her nigga; to know him was to love him.

"DING, DONG! DING DONG!" The bell sounded.

Even in her sleep, Brianna had heard the bell. She thought she was dreaming though. So she continued in her slumber.

"Ding Dong! Ding Dong!"

The sound of the doorbell shattered the silence of the house. Brianna knew that it wasn't a dream. Someone was at her front door. She wondered who it was. She hoped it wasn't the police coming to interrogate her again.

Slowly Brianna rose from her bed, gathering her bearings. She slipped on a large fluffy white bathrobe and a pair of Nike slippers, which had formally belonged to Tre, and headed downstairs to answer the door.

Ding Dong! Ding Dong! Ding Dong! The doorbell began to go berserk.

Just a few feet away from the door, Brianna's curiosity was suddenly over taken by anger. She wanted to know who the hell was ringing her doorbell like that.

"Who is it?" She barked.

There was no answer.

"Who is it?" She screamed again.

Brianna was on fire, somebody was at her front door playing games and she was not in the mood for it. All things considered.

Without thinking Brianna unbolted a series of locks and snatched the door open. To her surprise, Tre's aunt Angie and his cousin, her daughter Yvette stood in front of her. She was frozen at the sight of them.

Suddenly, Brianna's mood went from bad to worse. She knew that their appearance at her front door wasn't a goodwill mission. And they weren't there to offer their condolences.

"Good morning?" Angie greeted her. "You mind if we come in?"

Not waiting for a reply the two women barged right past Brianna.

"Come on in!" Brianna said sarcastically.

As soon as they entered the house, the two women began scanning the premises for valuables. As if it was an auction. No matter how hard they tried their eyes couldn't hide their intentions. They were like vultures on a dead carcass; they were there to pick the body clean.

To her credit Brianna already knew what it was. She had felt their vibe a few days ago at the funeral and everyday thereafter. She had expected them to show up. The only question was what had taken them so long?

"Damn! Ya'll was ballin' fa real." Yvette exclaimed, as she looked around the state of the art living room.

Brianna just stared at her blankly. She wasn't even going to dignify her with a response.

Brianna hadn't liked Yvette from day one. She had it out for her, Yvette tried and kept trying to put her girlfriends onto Tre. Over the years, they had had dozens of verbal altercations over the matter. Each side issued threats but never once did they come to fisticuffs, because Tre wouldn't allow it. Now that the peacemaker was gone, it was open season on Brianna.

Angie suddenly announced, "Look, Bri I'm goin' to cut right to the chase. The reason we're here is to pick up some things that my nephew Tre had promised me. He always told me, if anything ever happened to him that I could come over and take anything I wanted…"

Yvette replied, "Funny, he told me the same thing."

Brianna shot her a look that seemed to say, 'You-can't-be serious.'

She knew that Angie was lying through her teeth. Tre wasn't real close to anyone in his family, except his grandmother. He'd felt like his family was nothing but a bunch of leeches. No matter how much he gave them, they were never satisfied. They always had their hand out. In spite of that, he took care of them out of a sense of loyalty.

"Yeah, anyway!" Angie countered. "Since I was his favorite Auntie and everything, he said he would feel better if I had it."

"Oh yeah?" Brianna shot back with her arms folded across her breasts.

"Yeah!" Angie said with emphasis.

In the background, Brianna could see Yvette posturing with her hands on her hips. This provided Brianna only a hint of their collective foul mood. The sinister smirk that had spread across her lips seemed to tell it all.

The tension in the house was thick. At any minute violence could explode. Both parties took defiant stances, glaring at one another. Quickly Brianna weighted her odds, she ruled out striking Tre's aunt. She knew that if she fought one, then she would have to fight them both. And that they would most defiantly jump her. With these two ghetto dwellers there was no telling just how far they would go.

"Look, this shit don't mean nuttin' to me. Take whatever you want." She told them. "I'm in love with Tre! Not his possessions."

"Whatever, Bitch!" Yvette snapped, trying to instigate a fight.

Brianna shook her head in disgust; she took pity on these two savages. One of Tre's famous sayings suddenly came to mind. 'Don't become too attached to this shit. The drug game and life is so funny. What takes you years to get, can take you less than twenty minutes to lose.'

Brianna was in an awkward situation, on one hand she felt that she was entitled to everything. On the other, she felt indebted to Tre's family, but not these two, after all blood was thicker than water. She had only known him a few short years and they a lifetime.

A concession had to be made. Out of respect for Tre, Brianna decided not to make a big deal of it. The material items in the house could be gotten again, more expensive items at that. Still that notion didn't stop her ill feelings toward them. In her book they were just grimy. There was no other way to explain their actions.

Tre must be rolling over in his grave. She mused. Spurred by disappointment, Brianna went upstairs to her bedroom and locked the door. In silence she listened as the duo pillaged the house.

"Ohh, Mommy lemme have the microwave, you already got the blender." Yvette said.

Brianna listened intently as the two scavengers fought over who would get what. It was sad to see just how petty, two human beings could be. It was also disheartening to see just how death bought out the worst in people.

Upstairs in her bedroom Brianna paced the spacious room, back and forth like caged animal. She had to do something to rid herself of this nervous energy. She had to do something to keep herself from going back downstairs and jumping on somebody.

Impatiently she bided her time, in her bedroom, for what seemed like an eternity. Suddenly just as quickly as the commotion started, it came to an end. The quietness that engulfed the house was a sign to Brianna that the intruders were gone.

Quickly she went into her closet and opened a storage bin that was hidden way in the back. She pulled out a pair of old blue jeans and a bleached stained red t-shirt. In a hurried fashion, she put the clothes on. Then Brianna raced down stairs, through the house, into the backyard, it was time to dig up Tre's drug stash.

Tre wasn't too big on telling Brianna everything. Or any woman for that matter, he thought women were weak. If enough pressure was applied by law enforcement authorities, they would break. Tre didn't want to tempt fate. He always said 'what you don't know you can't tell.'

Fortunately over the years, he had grown comfortable with Brianna. He began to let her in on some of his secrets. Just in case anything ever happened to him. As it turned out this would be the most crucial one of all.

As soon as Brianna entered the backyard, she stood still. A puzzled look masked her face, as if she was trying to recall something. Scanning the yard she looked for a tool to assist her task. Leaning against the house she spotted a garden hoe. After taking the tool into her hands, she went about her business.

Retracing her steps, Brianna began her expedition at the back door. Slowly she took eight paces straight ahead, then made a sharp right and took four more paces. Where she stood, supposedly, x marked the spot. The dope was literally beneath her feet, buried in a shallow hole in the soft earth.

Burying this stash of dope was totally Tre's idea. He used to do this as a youth when he sold drugs out of a dope house. To avoid being robbed or caught by the police with large packages of drugs, he buried them in a nearby wooded area, taking only what he thought he could sell. This was a brilliant stroke of genius, not once did Tre loss a single gram, adhering to this system.

Brianna was sure that it was the right spot. With all her might, she brought the hoe down tearing away at the patches of grass. Powerful strokes from the hoe began to tear huge chunks of earth and grass. Soon Brianna began to break a sweat. She kicked away all the debris and fell to her knees. With her bare hands she began digging away like a dog. At a feverish pace, she attacked the earth as if it were a bitter enemy.

Brianna was glad it was still early, her neighbors most likely were at work and so no prying eyes would witness the extraction of drugs from the earth.

"God Damn!" She cursed. "Where the fuck is it?"

Just as Brianna was about to lose hope, her hands unearth some plastic. She breathed easy. She knew that was it. She watched Tre when he prepared the dope for burial. The sight of the package of dope spurred her on. She began to dig with a renewed vigor.

Finally Brianna excavated the package of dope, it was taped and double tapped, then wrapped in plastic, to protect it from the elements. She didn't even bother to brush off the leftover particles of dirt. She merely clutched the package to her chest and rush inside her house.

As she begin tearing open the package. She couldn't believe how many lives had been destroyed for this white powder. She also didn't realize the worth of what she had in her possession. There was so much tape to tear through she began to get tired all over again. She decided to put the packages in her closet until she could figure out what she would do next. Brianna knew she had to figure out how and who to move them too.

Buzz, buzz, buzz. Where is that sound coming from Brianna thought to herself. She looked over on Tre's nightstand to see his cell phone vibrating off the stand onto the floor. She hurried and picked the phone up. Looking at the outer display it read Jason. Brianna knew that Jason was one of Tre's out of town clientele. He was a southern hustler out of the ATL. She didn't know if the news had reached that far of Tre's death. So she decided to answer the phone.

"Hello."

"What Up Bri? Where Tre at?"

Hearing someone ask for Tre threw Brianna off, as she thought to herself he must not know.

"He's not here right now, I'll tell him you called Jason."

"Aight Bri, let him know I need to holla at him, a nigga dry down here."

"Ok I will let him know" with that Brianna hung up the phone, knowing that she had solved the problem of who, now it was just a matter of how.

Chapter Four

YOU CAN FIND ME IN THE A

I nterstate 85 seemed to be infested with marked and unmarked patrol cars for a Sunday afternoon. Brianna set the cruise control on the rental car at 65 mph, nevertheless she still kept her mind and senses alert. After continuously receiving calls from Jason about needing work down in the Atl, Brianna finally devised a plan to move some of the work that was left in Tre's stash ... Completely green to the financial side of the dope game she set out on the first of what would be one of many journeys to Atlanta Georgia ...

"THANK YOU TRE ... thank you ... thank you ... thank you," Brianna said aloud to the many photos still hanging throughout the home they had once shared. Four weeks ago she didn't know how she was gonna make it. Tre's family had damn near stripped her home of everything but their bedroom set. She didn't even have a television to watch. Once again she took a deep breath, sighed and gave thanks to her long lost love, as she stared at over eighty thousand dollars strolled out all over her bed. After Tre's death Brianna was left only a few options.

She could've laid in that townhouse and starved to death or went back home to her mother and continued to take the abuse of an unforgiving step- father. She chose neither. After all the pain and suffering she went through during her loss, Brianna felt as if everybody had turned their backs on her and Tre and gave them their asses to kiss; especially his materialistic family. Not to mention his so-called boys.

She knew she had to take all the knowledge Tre had schooled her with about the dope game, and everything else she learned along the way. She had been soaking up the gritty ways of the streets like an overly eager adolescent still in grade school, and now it was time for graduation.

Buzz ... Buzz ... Buzz ... Tre's cell phone vibrated steadily against Brianna's mid-section startling her from her temporary daydream. Checking the number display, she saw that it was Tre's best friend "Havok" calling again. Havok, whose real name was Hakeem, grew up in the same neighborhood as Tre. They had been inseparable as teenagers, going to war together against other neighborhood gangs. It seemed as if nothing could come between them. That was until Petey pulled Tre in under his wing. Petey's big brother bond with Tre slowly drove an invisible wedge between him and Havok's friendship. Havok despised Petey. Never once did he offer to let Havok tag along with him and Tre. Making matters worse was the fact that he was fucking his favorite auntie. Havok's aunt, Dez, short for Deserae was like a second mother to him. She was beautiful by anyone's standards. She had been voted Prom Queen in high school and predicted as one who would most likely succeed in life. "Dez" had it all, beauty, brains and most of all she carried herself with elegance and style. Even though she had witnessed several of her classmates and friends suffer through broken marriages, abortions and fall victim of the streets, Dez had dreams; dreams of making it out of the projects. But as fate would have it, her dreams fell on the shoulders of an up and coming trap-star with nothing more than a hustler's mentality.

"Yes," Brianna said answering Tre's phone:

"Wassup Bri ... How you feeling today? ..."

"I'm cool, Hakeem," Brianna answered calling him by his government name.

"Yo, you don't sound cool," he said.

"We'll how do you expect me to feel? My man ain't never coming back ..." Brianna said, her voice breaking up. She continued, "Damn Hakeem I know this shit may sound crazy to you but, I can still feel Tre's presence in this house."

Hakeem could hear Brianna's voice starting to break-up again over the phone so he quickly changed the subject.

"Look Bri ... I'm almost done here so get dressed alight."

"Done where, and get dressed for what Hakeem?" she asked. "I'm at the car wash on Betty's Ford," he answered.

Bri sat quietly for a moment thinking to herself ... Betty's Ford Road Carwash ... She remembered her and Tre had stopped through there the same day they were robbed. The car wash was an all night hang out spot for all types of criminals. Every drug-dealer in the city got their cars detailed by the dope fiends who hung out there 24/7.

"Brianna ... Brianna ... Whassup, are you still there?" Hakeem yelled into the phone.

"Yeah ... yes I'm still here Hakeem," Brianna answered. Her mind cloudy and confused.

"Get dressed," he told her once again.

"Alright, give me an hour." Brianna told him before ending their call.

After closing her phone, Brianna headed towards her laundry room. She struggled to pull the dryer away from the wall and lifted a small portion of the floor revealing a large safe. She quickly opened it and tossed the eighty thousand dollars inside then locked it, pushing the heavy dryer back in its place.

Brianna showered and got dressed, then flopped down on the new lamb skin sofa she'd brought a few days ago, along with a 61" plasma flat screen TV. Her trips back and forth to Atlanta had given her very little time to enjoy any of the new items she'd purchased. But that was only a fraction of Brianna's problem. Her biggest problem was no longer money or any of the materialistic things. No, Brianna Campbell's biggest problem was the empty void that was left in her life after Tre's death. She stared back and forth at all the pictures throughout their home. Whether with her or his boys, Tre always displayed his trademark smile which seemed to go perfect with his short fade.

Brianna reached for a picture of Tre sitting in front of her on the small table. It was a photo of him and his best friend Hakeem at the club. Tre and Hakeem did everything together like they were identical twin brothers. Sitting there holding Tre's picture, Brianna found herself sobbing again.

"Baby how am I going to make it without you?" she mumbled out loud. "I wish you were here Tre, I ..."

Ding Dong ... Ding Dong ... Ding Dong ... Brianna's sobs were interrupted by the sound of the door-bell.

She sighed heavily remembering that Hakeem was on the way over. Brianna pulled herself together and wiped away the tears as best she could then prepared to answer the door.

After making sure that it was indeed Hakeem she opened the door. To her surprise Hakeem was holding a life size teddy bear in one arm and a dozen red roses in the other.

Brianna stared at the teddy-bear and roses which, once again, brought back bitter-sweet memories of Tre. When she'd moved in with him Brianna told Tre all about her troubled childhood. As a little girl all she wanted for Christmas and birthdays was a teddy-bear and a close knit family to share her dreams with. Since her stepfather wouldn't allow her mother to spend a dime on her, she'd never gotten any of those things. It had taken her days before she was able to talk

Tre out of killing her stepfather. One day Brianna returned home from a hair appointment and found their home flooded with all types of teddy Bears and flowers.

"They're for you," Hakeem said, interrupting Brianna's thoughts.

"Oh ... AAh ... I can't accept that Hakeem I ..." "Come on Brianna it's nothing," he said cutting her off. "Besides, Tre told me how much you liked 'em," he continued while handing her the fluffy white teddy-bear.

Brianna hesitated a moment longer before finally accepting the gifts.

"Thank you Hakeem, they're beautiful," Brianna said rubbing the soft fur on the teddy-bears ears.

"Are you ready to bounce," he asked.

"Yeah. Just give me a minute to put these flowers in some water," she answered.

Five minutes later, they prepared to leave.

"So where are we going Hakeem?" Brianna asked.

"I thought we would just grab something to eat," he answered.

Hakeem opened the passenger door to the two door platinum Masarati coupe. Brianna remembered the day he brought the car by the house to show it to Tre. She remembered hearing the heated argument about his new purchase.

"Damn my nigga I told you about buying this all eyes on me shit. You just putting a bull's eye on your back for the Feds and the stick up kids!"

"Man fuck that! I'm going to live my life, this shit can all end tomorrow. Jail or death don't mean shit to me, as long as mother fuckers remember my name!" Hakeem had responded.

"Well don't bring that hot shit by my house, you do what you do over your way! And how you going to be asking a nigga to throw you some doe for your case and you out here buying new shit?"

"Nigga one thang don't have nothing to do with the other, I just need to borrow that little bit of bread to give to my lawyer. He already told me

that for $80,000.00 he can have all charges dropped. Then I will give you back your little money!" Hakeem screamed back.

"Look bro you know I got love for you like family. So I'm going to keep it 100 with you. I had my attorney look into your case and he told me it's no way you walk away without doing some time. That lawyer of yours is just trying to beat you for your money and he using you not wanting to go to jail to do it."

"Man fuck that! And fuck your attorney! If you don't want to let me hold the money just say that!

"Bro you know it's not like that" Tre had a concern look on his face. "Look my nigga I will give you half of it and you come up with the rest, that's the best I can do!" Tre extended his hand out to Hakeem. Hakeem grabbed it and they went into a man hug, touching chest.

Aight Tre that's whats up, I guess I just got to figure out how to get the other part.

"Nigga sell this car! Or one of your cars or some of that jewelry" Tre said while trying not to laugh. His smile made Hakeem break out into one also.

"Aight my nigga let me get out of here, you see Bri sitting in the car and we got dinner reservations. Shit holla at me tomorrow."

"Are you okay Bri?" Hakeem asked interrupting her thought.

"Oh ... AAh ... I'm okay," she replied.

Several minutes later, they pulled up at Brianna's favorite restaurant, Flemings, located in downtown Charlotte's EpiCenter. After throwing the keys to the valet, she and Hakeem were seated in the restaurant.

"So Bri, I just wanted to let you know that Tre was my nigga. And when I find out who did this to you... these niggas going to die a slow death. I also know he wouldn't want you sitting around doing nothing with the rest of the life you been blessed with. So what are your plans?"

In truth Brianna had not thought about the rest of her life. She was only concerned with the here and now. She took a small piece of the lamb chops she had ordered into her mouth.

"You know Hakeem, I have not thought about it. But I'm sure I will figure something out."

"I'm sure you will Bri, my nigga always said how smart you were, so I know you will be ok. I just want to let you know if you need anything. Don't hesitate to call me."

"Thanks Hakeem, I appreciate everything you have done. I could have never planned out Tre's funeral. Are you sure I don't owe you anything? I know it wasn't cheap."

"Stop it girl, one thing you got to remember about me, is that money ain't thang. I spend it like it comes… fast! Plus like I told you that was my nigga!"

Chapter Five

A TRAP-STAR IS BORN

The Westin Hotel hadn't changed much since the last time Brianna had been there. A year ago she and Tre had celebrated New Years in one of the large suites overlooking the city.

"Damn," she mumbled to herself as she approached the registers desk.

"May I help you," asked a heavyset lady sitting behind the counter.

"Carlos Garcia's room please," Brianna answered.

"AAh ... Mr. Garcia,'" the lady repeated with a sudden smile.

"Miss Campbell I assume."

"Yes," Brianna said flashing her own smile.

"Right this way Miss Campbell, Mr. Garcia is expecting you."

Brianna followed the woman into what looked to be an empty dining area. At least she thought it was empty until a middle aged man who seemed to have appeared from out of nowhere approach her. The lady who'd escorted her to him.

"Miss Campbell," the man said in a heavily accented deep

voice, which seemed to vibrate throughout the entire dining area.

Brianna shyly nodded her.

"May I?" he asked reaching for her hand.

She said yes with a nod of her head.

The man gently caressed Brianna's hand before kissing it softly.

"Greetings Miss Campbell, my boss is expecting you."

After leading her to a nearby table, the gentleman prepared to leave.

Brianna took notice of the man as she took a seat at the table. He had a nasty looking scar, which began just below the left temple and ended just above his juggler vein.

"Carlos will be with you momentarily," the man said interrupting her thoughts.

"Thank you," Brianna said before he turned and silently walked away.

She sat quietly alone in the dining area, which was a little top quiet for her taste.

Her mind suddenly drifting back two days ago to when she'd received the call that had added more confusion to her already complicated life.

After showering, Brianna had just snuggled underneath the covers in her bedroom. It had been a long day. The clock read 4:00a.m. Returning from a long trip to Atlanta, all Brianna could imagine during the ride was lying in her bed sleeping for the next 24 hours. Jason had bought the last four kilos she had left from Tre's stash. After her third drop off with him, Brianna finally told him about Tre's death. For the first time since his murder Brianna saw someone besides herself show some type of visible emotion. Jason was heartbroken. He told Brianna that before her first trip he knew something was wrong. He had figured Tre had probably gotten arrested and was being held on some type of large bond, and that Brianna, being a true "hustler's wife," was out getting the paper up to get her man out of jail. Sadly, that wasn't the case.

"Yes," Brianna said in a groggy voice answering Tre's cell phone.

"Greetings Brianna, I hate to bother you at such an hour but I ..."

"Who the hell is this," Brianna asked with an attitude.

"I'm a very good friend of Treshawn."

"A friend."

"Yes, I'm a friend," he repeated again.

"If you're a friend of Treshawn's Mr. ... AAh ... what is your name anyway?" Brianna asked.

"Carlos ... Carlos Garcia," he answered.

"Well Carlos," she blurted out loudly. *"What the hell do you want at this time of morning?*

My apologies it is day time in my country, me and Tre were, how do say um.., business partners."

Business partners. It didn't take long for Brianna to process a Spanish accent, different time zone, and business partner. This had to be Tre's connect!

"Can we meet?" he asked her directly.

"Do I have a choice or is that an order?" she countered.

"We always have a choice, but I think it would be in your best interest to at least hear me out. I will be in your city in two days and we can talk more in-depth!"

"AAh Brianna I see you made it," a well-dressed Hispanic man said walking ever so gently up to her table.

"Carlos Garcia," he said.

"Brianna Campbell," she responded.

"So Mr. Garcia how do yo ..."

"Please Brianna, call me Carlos," he said interrupting her.

"Okay, Mr. Carlos how can I help you?"

He paused a moment, his mind filtering the question he'd been asked.

"First let me say Tre was like a son to me, and to hear of his death was truly heart breaking. However business is business and there are some matters to clear up."

Brianna began to get nervous. She never thought about having to answer for the money or the drugs. This was the other side of the game she was not aware of.

"There is a matter of half a million dollars that is due to me. Now let me say that I am well aware of your recent transaction on Tre's behalf in Atlanta. And I have no problem with you continuing to handle that situation. However, debts must be covered. It's just business."

Brianna began to speak with a slight quiver in her voice. "I don't have a half a million I don't even have half of that half a million. I've only made about $250,000.00."

Carlos began to crack a smile "Brianna I am not an unreasonable or impassionate man. I understand that bills had to be paid. What I propose now is a payment plan where we both can continue to do business and prosper. All you need to do is continue to make your trips and I will make sure you have all the product you need. With the rate you been working thus far, it won't take long to cover that small debt.

By the look on Carlos' face, there was not an option in this matter, rather an instruction. The truth was, Brianna didn't have anything else going on in her life. The trips to see Jason had been easy enough, she thought. Plus she was making enough money to keep up the life style she had become so accustomed to.

Over dinner, Carlos informed her when and where the product would arrive, and where to send his payments to. If she followed all his instruction there would be no problems. And just like Tre had done, she would be well taken care of.

Chapter Six

"A STAR IS BORN"

O
n the way home from the meeting, Brianna scrolled through her phone list. She needed someone to talk to; someone that she could trust to share her experience with Carlos with. Tre had always been the one person in her life she could talk to about anything. Her eyes became glossy with tears, as they always did these days when Tre crossed her mind. She blinked them away; this was no time to be weak. She knew that the only way she would be successful at taking over Tre's work would be to maintain her composure and always appear strong.

Her finger scrolled its way to Hakeem's number. She hesitated. Insecurities flooded her mind. Maybe the only reason Hakeem had kept her company was as a last favor to Tre. She figured that he probably didn't really want anything to do with her long term. Brianna pressed the end button on her phone and threw it on the passenger seat of her car. Press forward. Stay strong. Hold your head up high. You can do this alone. She repeated theses things herself over and over again as she headed towards home.

Brianna stepped off the elevator to her new condo. Walking in a room where the love of her life had been murdered, and where she'd been left for dead had only heightened the emotional roller coaster she'd been on since Tre's death. She liked this new place equip with floor to ceiling windows, hardwood floors, granite countertops, stainless steel appliances, and a view that could kill. Plus, there was a 24-hour front desk concierge that offered the extra layer of security that she needed. There was a mirror directly in front of the elevator doors. Brianna looked herself and smiled with pride. She was, after all, more than her stepfather ever said she would be. As she turned the corner, she noticed a male figure standing in the front of her place with his ear cuffing the door. She started to panic almost immediately. Brianna slowly backed away towards the elevator. She pressed the down button rapidly. The numbers lit up while the elevator slowly made it's way back to her. As the elevator paused on a lower floor, Brianna heard footsteps. She kicked herself for wanting to be on the top floor. She bowed her head and allowed her hair to cover her face.

"Brianna?" a familiar voice inquired.

She looked up and into the smiling face of Hakeem.

She smile, "Hey."

"Hey, you leaving back out? I was just coming by to check on you."

"Oh, I ahhh…" she shook her head, "No, I thought I left something in the car. It can stay."

Hakeem walked close to her and reached his arms out for a hug. Brianna wrapped her arms around his torso. He looked at her and shook his head, then repositioned her arms around his neck. He moved close to her body, wrapping his arms around her petite waist and squeezed tight.

She had been affection deprived. Brianna felt herself nearly collapse into his arms. If felt good to be embraced, so good that she leaned in closer. Right when she started feeling comfortable, Hakeem loosened his grip.

"I was just coming to check on you. Hoping you'd be up for a movie night."

The pair walked to Brianna's condo. She noticed that by the door, Hakeem had left a couple dvd's, a box of microwaveable popcorn, and a variety of chocolate candy bars.

"Oh, wow. This is a nice surprise." Brianna unlocked the door and welcomed Hakeem in. "I'd love a movie night. Have a seat, let me get comfortable."

"Aiight, cool. I'll set up the movie in here."

Brianna went into her room to change into something comfortable. She traded out her black patent leather Louboutin pumps for fuzzy white slippers, her jeans and Bebe blouse for her Victoria Secret Pink sweat pants and tee. She pulled her hair back into a low ponytail, and headed back to the living room.

"Thanks again for coming by. How's your day been?"

"It's been ok. How about you?"

"No complaints. I'm coming from a meeting so it'll be nice to relax."

"A meeting, huh?"

"Yeah, a meeting... well more like an interview."

"Oh yeah? You tryna get a 9 to 5? I thought for sure Tre woulda had you set tight."

"Yeah, but I still gotta stay afloat once that runs out. I can't live forever off of what he left me."

"So how'd the interview go?"

"Pretty good. I got the job," she smiled.

"Congratulations!"

"Thanks! What movies did you pick up?" she asked trying to change the subject.

"I got some old school stuff..."

Hakeem always had a crush on Brianna. From the day Tre introduced them he had taken notice of her. He found it appealing that a girl as attractive as her seemed to not even realize it. Since high school, Hakeem and Tre had developed a recycling system with the girls they dated and slept with. Once one was finished, the other would swoop in to play the knight in shining armor and pick up where the other had left off. It worked like a charm every time. For years Hakeem had been waiting in the sidelines for Tre to be done with Brianna so he could take his turn, but as each year passed it became apparent that she was different. And Brianna never really seemed to notice him anyway. In Hakeem's mind, she was the female version of Petey. When Petey was killed, he was back to being Tre's sidekick, but that only lasted for a short time once things got serious with Brianna. It was always all about Tre.

One night Tre took his whole crew to VIP at On the Roxx to celebrate Brianna's birthday. One of Tre's partners Fresh had thrown a huge party for her. Hakeem thought that it was the best he'd ever seen her look. She wore a fitted black romper that accentuated her every curve. Her hair draped her shoulders in big curls that danced as she moved to the music. The only other woman in the room that even came close to competing with her was her little sister, Charrise, who wore a fitted pink dress and her hair pulled back into a ponytail. Tre had introduced the two, but Hakeem was mesmerized by Brianna. When she excused herself to go to the restroom, Tre caught Hakeem checking Brianna out. Tre sat back and watched his best friend practically raping her with his eyes. Tre made a mental note of this; he knew Hakeem had a liking for her. So he made sure from that point on to not tell him about his and Brianna relationship. He could hear the words of Petey speaking to him "Don't ever trust any man alone with your woman, not even me!"

Tre walked up on Hakeem from behind and said, "Nigga what the fuck are you lookin' at?"

Hakeem was startled, "Oh it's like that? You trippin over this broad. A nigga can't even look at her without you actin' like a bitch? You should be flattered!"

"Who the fuck is you talkin to like that?"

Hakeem turned and faced him, "What you mean who am I talkin to? You nigga!"

Tre balled up his fist, but held his composure. "You bitch ass nigga, you better keep your eyes on your own shit and stay off mine!"

"Word?" Hakeem shook his head and laughed it off, "I hear you nigga."

From that point on, Hakeem was real careful about how he looked at Brianna.

Brianna and Hakeem sat on opposite ends of the sofa while Coming to America played. Brianna sat with her knees curled up underneath her. She could feel him staring at her. She looked at him and asked, "What's up? Why you lookin at me like that?"

He shook his head, "My bad. I'm just worried about you. You've been through a lot lately."

"I'll be aiight."

"I know you will," he said while scooting over closer to her. "We fam, you don't have sit allllll the way over there like we're strangers," he laughed.

Once Hakeem's body was flush up against Brianna's he put his arm around her.

"You know, Tre always told me that if anything ever happened to him to look out for you. And that's exactly what I'm gonna do. You can feel comfortable with me."

Brianna sat speechless with her eyes glued to the television screen. Even though she didn't affirm it to him, it felt good to know that she wasn't alone, and that she had someone to lean on. She allowed the tension to leave her shoulder, and she relaxed into his arms.

Brianna's eyes slowly crept open early the next morning. She lay on her side on the sofa. She looked down and saw an arm draped over her. She looked ahead and saw several pieces of jewelry that were not her own sitting on the coffee table.

When she turned her head to the side she had to brush away the dreads that had settled on her cheek. There she was being spooned by her dead boyfriend's best friend. Surprisingly it felt good to not sleep alone. Even though this body was unfamiliar to her, and nothing like that of Tre's, it still felt comforting. Brianna sat up and stretched; with a glance over her shoulder she noticed that Hakeem was also awake.

"Good Morning," he said.

"Good Morning," she responded.

And awkward silence lingered between them. Brianna stood up and busied herself straightening up the living room.

Hakeem broke the silence, "Movie night was cool, maybe we can do it again sometime?"

Brianna nodded.

"I'ma get up outta here. Gotta meeting with my attorney."

"Is everything ok?"

"Yeah, it's cool. I just beat this case, but got some follow-up details to attend to."

Hakeem took a minute to replace his necklace, watch, and rings. Then he reached out for a goodbye hug. On his way out he said, "You know I got you right?"

"Yeah."

"For real. I got you. You need anything, I'm the one you should call first." He reiterated.

"Thanks," she smiled and locked the door behind him.

After Hakeem left, Brianna got on the phone immediately. It was time to get back to business.

"Hey Jason. I got some more work for ya."

"Aiight shorty. When can I expect you?'

"I'm finna hit the road shortly. I'll call you when I'm there."

Brianna pulled the Hertz rental car into her storage unit. Thanks to Carlos she had been schooled with key information to make these trips as safe as possible. After shutting the storage door, she hit the trunk symbol on the key pad. She removed the spare tire and placed a pen in the vale stem to release the air. The tire was about half empty, when she began to place the drugs inside.

' Ok that was easy enough" she thought to herself, as she replaced the tire and shut the trunk. She put in her favorite Beyonce CD and was ready to ride.

Brianna had driven this route so many times with Tre. She knew the process by heart. She didn't think that Tre ever realized how much attention she was paying. Until now, she hadn't even realized it herself. She had picked up where he left off seamlessly thus far. She remembered the rules of the game. The goal was to drive amongst everyone else without looking at all suspicious. No flashy car or clothes. Just a regular girl going on a regular trip. She dressed accordingly. Jeans, basic white tee, and sneakers. Brianna left her hair hanging at her shoulders and put on a pair of shades. On the road again.

The Ritz-Carlton in downtown Atlanta always welcomed Brianna with open arms and comfortable beds. Instead of the suite that she and Tre usually booked, a simple room with a King sized bed was enough for a solo Brianna. More often than not Brianna's days were filled with silence. She thought back on her night with Hakeem and smiled. It felt natural to spend time with him alone, even though they hadn't been close before Tre's passing. Tre had always seemed to be annoyed or frustrated with Hakeem for one thing or another. Brianna often wondered why they were best friends at all. They were so different. Tre was cool, calm, and collected in the way he ran his business and personal life. Hakeem, or Havok as his friends called him, on the other hand made a splash everywhere he went. Brianna laughed to herself thinking about how he'd showed up at events wearing a Gucci hat, matching belt, and shoes. He'd have the loudest music blaring from whatever flamboyant car he was driving at the time.

After settling in Brianna got to work and called Jason, "Meet me at the spot in fifteen."

"Aiight."

Brianna drove about 15 minutes to Lennox Mall. She pulled up and placed the rental car were it would be easily noticed. As she was walking in the mall, two guys were coming out the door. The short dark skin one grabbed her arm.

"What's Up Shorty? What you doing shopping by yourself?"

Brianna nicely grabbed his hand to release hers. "I'm not, I'm meeting my boyfriend for lunch."

"Well you let that nigga know he a lucky and here my card if he act up."

"Well thank you and I will keep the card." She plastered a fake smile on her face. There was a time when Brianna would have cursed him out for putting his hands on her. But she knew this was not the time to draw any attention. So diplomacy was the best option. She continued on through the door and made her way to the food court where Jason was already seated.

"What up, Bri? You want anything to eat or drink?"

"No I'm good, I got to get back to Charlotte."

"I feel you, well the car is a red mustang, and it's parked on the second level about six rows down."

"Boy what I told you about these sports cars, you going to make me get a ticket on the way back." Brianna said with a slight laugh.

"Well what you got a nigga in today?"

"A white Chevy Malibu, you can't miss it, it's on the front row in the deck."

When Brianna got into the Mustang she realized she had left her CD in the other car. "Oh well, I will have to stop at Best Buy and grab me another one on the way back. When she arrived back at the hotel, Brianna hurried to her room to grab her belongings so she could head back to Charlotte. Her phone began to ring as she was packing the car. She looked at the caller ID and saw it was Jason.

"I know I left my CD in the car, you can give it to one of your hoodrats," Brianna said while laughing.

"Na that's not why I'm hitting you Bri. You just put too much sugar in my coffee. I can't drank all that shorty!"

Brianna caught on immediately, she knew he was telling her he couldn't move all the dope she had giving him.

"For real? Well how much do you generally like?"

"I can take six cubes for now. Get at me in a few weeks about more."

Brianna was left with over half of the product that she was expected to sell to pay off her debt. She didn't even know who else she could sell to. It seemed like all of Tre's other connects had found other ways to get their good because she hadn't received any other calls.

Without any options, Brianna drove back to her hotel suite and ordered room service for one. She knew that it was time for her to expand her budding business and start to generate some contacts of her own. She just had to find out how.

Chapter Seven

PERFECT TIMING

Brianna fished for her Blackberry in her Dolce & Gabbana handbag. She pulled it out to reveal a caller id picture of her asleep in Hakeem's arms. He had the biggest grin on his face. She shook her head and smiled.

"Hey silly!" she said.

"What's good?"

"I see you took the liberty of making some changes to my phone."

He laughed, "Yeah. You don't mind do you?"

"Nah, how are you today? How'd things go with your attorney?"

"Truthfully, not so good." He explained, "My money is looking tight right now and that's exactly what I need to stay out of prison. Since Tre passed, I haven't been eating like normal so…"

"I hadn't even thought about that." She said more to herself than to him. It was like a light bulb had gone off in her head. "I don't' know why I didn't think of that before."

"Huh? What's up?"

"I think I can help you with your problem, and you can help me with a problem I have."

"Okay... how so? Did Tre leave some food you need to get rid of?"

"Ummm, not quite. Meet me for lunch. I need to fill you in on some things."

Hakeem and Brianna met at Chima's in downtown Charlotte. As they began looking over the choices of Brazilin foods. Brianna started to explain the steps she had taken since Tre's death.

"That interview I was telling you about the other day was actually a meeting with Carlos, Tre's connect. Right now I only have one person picking up work from me, but I've got a lot left. So basically, I'm the new Tre... you need work and I've got it."

Hakeem smiled. This was just what he needed to put himself back in the game. On top of that partnering with Brianna would work to his advantage. She could keep the connect with Carlos, but he'd play the main man in the streets. While Brianna would actually be the true Tre replacement, no one in the streets would really know that. In the streets he'd be the main man taking over Tre's position.

He sat back in his chair and nodded, "Aiight, I'm down."

Buzz... Buzz... her sister's number and picture displayed on the screen of her phone. Charrise was the only person from her family that she had kept in contact with since she moved out. She had never been close with her brother; he had copied after his father in the way he treated his older sister. Brianna didn't know if she would ever forgive her mother for allowing her to be treated so badly all those years. But Charrise had always been her one ally in the house.

"What's up?" Brianna asked with an attitude.

"What's your problem," Charrise retorted.

"I ain't heard from you since Tre died. What's up with that?"

Charrise exhaled, "Girl, you don't even know. A lot's been going on over here."

"So that means you can't call and check on your sister?"

"My bad. I'm sorry. We need to talk. Can I come over?"

"Yeah, but I moved. I'll text you the address."

An hour later, Charrise was knocking on the door. She strolled in looking like she had just had a hard day's work, and Brianna knew that couldn't be the case. As the true first baby girl of Herman, Charrise had rarely lifted a finger growing up. She was doted on like a princess with no regard or concern for the effect this imbalance of treatment would have on Brianna. In secret, Charrise would share nearly all of her goodies with her older sister. They shared everything except clothes and shoes. It only took one time for the girls to learn that wasn't a good idea. When their father saw Brianna in one of the outfits he'd purchased for Charrise, he made her undress immediately. He said, "Since you wanna wear other people's clothes we'll be getting yours from the Goodwill from now on."

To take it a step further he went to the Goodwill himself to pick out the items, making sure to get things that were out of style and tacky. He came home with bags and bags of the ugliest clothes Brianna had ever seen. It was her first year of junior high school and that shabby gear earned her the nickname Bri-tacky. That nickname followed her through her senior year, even after he'd allowed her mother to resume her shopping at regular stores.

"What's going on?" Brianna asked.

"Girrrrl," Charrise started dramatically, "Daddy's restaurants are being closed down."

"Umph," Brianna shrugged, "Why should I care?"

"I know, I know… you hate him, but just hear me out. Turns out he hasn't been paying his taxes and the IRS finally caught up with him. We're only operating out of one location, he had to fire all of the staff and now, it's only me, momma, and Jonathan working for him."

"Damn! For real."

"For real! I'm sick of this shit! He's as mean as ever now…

been talkin' to momma any old kinda way. Putting down Jonathan... he even went off on me the other day. This stress really has him going crazy!"

"Now y'all know how I felt all those years."

"I guess... but we need your help."

"We? Who the hell is we?"

"Ok... let me rephrase... I need your help."

"I'm not doing anything that involves helping that man!"

"Don't do it for him... do it for me. Your sister... the rest of us are suffering for his mistakes. I don't have anybody else to ask."

"For the record, it wasn't just him. Momma never stood up for me... and Jonathan... don't even get me started on Jonathan."

Charrise scooted close to her sister. She pouted and put on her puppy dog eyes. "Please. I'm begging you... and you know I do not beg! Help your sister out."

"HOW MUCH DO YOU NEED?"

"A few thousand... like thirty."

"What makes you think I have that kind of money sitting around?"

Charrise took a minute to observe her surroundings making a mental inventory of the expensive things Brianna had decorated her new condo with. Over the fire place there was a 65 inch HDTV. The white, tufted sofa was flanked on either sided with mirrored side tables. Brianna had hardwood floors, and custom area rugs. Beautiful canvas paintings with pops of purple hung on the walls in the room.

"Brianna, who are you kidding? It's pretty obvious that Tre left you with some money. It doesn't look like your cash flow is hurting one bit."

"I need a drink," Brianna walked over to the wet-bar on the other side of the room and poured herself a glass of wine.

"Despite what you might think Charrise, I'm not in any position to give away that kind of money."

Charrise shook her head, "I should have known you wouldn't give it to me."

"You're absolutely right. Tre worked hard for what he had! And he worked hard to make sure I had what I needed. Why the fuck would I just be willing to give away anything? Especially for a family that doesn't give a shit about me!"

"Aiight, I get it. You don't have to get all hype with me."

"My bad... you know I get worked up about this family shit. Listen, because it's you asking, I think we can work something out. I'm not willing to give away anything, but you can absolutely work for it."

"YOU WANT ME TO DO WHAT?" Charrise asked with disgust coating her every word.

After a night of treating her sister to mani's and pedi's Brianna broke down the details of Charrise's new job description. They'd spent the night together, slumber party style. Wearing colorful pj's and sleeping side by side, after giggling over silly childhood memories. That morning they were talking about entering a life of crime.

Hakeem had come by ready to get to work. They all sat at the dining room table talking and eating over the breakfast Brianna had prepared. It'd been awhile since she'd had anyone to cook for, so she went all out. Blueberry pancakes, bacon, sausage, scrambled eggs, grits, fruit salad, and hash browns.

"That's the job. You want it or not?" Brianna said matter of factly.

"I came down here to this big ol' breakfast. I thought you were gonna announce that we'd go into the restaurant business ourselves or something. I don't know if I can do that. What if I get caught?"

Between bites, Hakeem jumped in, "You won't. It's real simple. Believe me."

Charrise shook her head, "I don't know why you just wouldn't give me the money."

Brianna rolled her eyes, "Listen, you DO already know why I won't just give you the money. If you keep playin' I'll take away the offer and you can figure it out for yourself. There are a lot of girls out here that would take this offer in a second! Getting paid just to do a few trips from Charlotte and ATL. Shit, I'm basically giving it away."

"I ain't never done nothing like this Bri."

"Neither had I before I did it the first time. I wouldn't have you do something that I wouldn't do myself. Look at me, I'm fine. Living in a nice home, driving a nice car, got plenty shoppin' money. Plus, you can move out of Mom and Dad's and move in here with me so they won't be asking you any questions."

Charrise looked up at her sister with a smile, "I can move in?"

"Yea."

Hakeem interjected again once his plate was clean, "And, since you so nervous, I can link you up with some of my partners down there. They'll look out for you and make sure everything goes seamless."

"Thanks Hakeem," Brianna said smiling at him.

"That's Havok when we're doing business," he said with a wink.

"Aiight, aiight. Thanks Havok."

"So, Charrise, what's it gonna be?"

"I'll do it."

Charrise finished her plate and headed to the room to shower and change. Brianna focused her attention on Hakeem.

"Ok now, Havok. It's time for you and I to handle some business. Now you know I want to look out for you as much as possible. However, Carlos has already told me to never front more than I can cover because ultimately, I'm responsible for the money. So you tell me how much you need and what you can prepay for and I'll put the rest on your face. Also, I will be throwing you something for your assistance with the ATL situation as a bonus. Now, is there anything you need from me?"

"Baby I just need you to get all you can get and I will handle the rest. The streets are so dry right now, that we can get all that work off this week!"

Satisfied with their agreement, Brianna cleared the table and went into the kitchen. She ran the hot water, rinsing off each dish before bending down to place them into the dishwasher. She didn't even hear Hakeem enter the kitchen, but she definitely felt her own temperature rise as his body grazed her from behind. She stood up and he kissed her neck, her body immediately responded with an arch in her back.

He whispered in her ear, "Damn girl. It's so sexy... you taking charge like that. I love a woman with some authority."

She turned her face a little and he met her lips with a kiss. He placed his hand on her face and pushed her lips even closer to his. She opened her mouth, allowing his tongue to enter. Brianna turned her body to face him. While his one hand cupped her butt, he slid the other under her shirt towards her breast. Her nipples hardened in anticipation. Hakeem pushed Brianna flush with the cabinets and pulled her shirt all the way up. He smiled. She wasn't wearing a bra. He went right for her nipple, tasting it and sucking it like a newborn baby. Brianna pressed her breast further into his mouth and threw her head back. It had been too long since she'd felt this type of arousal, and her body was yearning for it.

Just as Hakeem started to tug at her leggings, Brianna heard the voice of her sister calling for her.

"Bri! Where you at?"

Quickly Brianna pushed Hakeem away and pulled down her shirt.

"Brrrrrrrri!"

She turned back towards the sink and resumed rinsing dishes before yelling out, "In the kitchen."

Hakeem gave Brianna a quick slap on the ass, "I'm out. We'll finish this later."

Brianna was speechless. She hadn't seen this coming, but judging from the dampness between her legs, it was long overdue.

Charrise walked into the kitchen and said, "I'll be back. Gonna go get my things from home so I can move in. See ya later roomie."

Brianna cleared her throat. "You mean boss."

"Whatever… you gotta key for me?"

"Look in my nightstand."

Once the condo was empty, Brianna got in the shower and finished what Hakeem had started. It wasn't quite the same… but bringing herself to orgasm was better than nothing.

Chapter Eight

EVERY MAN FOR HIMSELF AND GOD FOR US ALL

Just as her sister had done several times, Charrise headed south on I-85. She had followed her sister's instructions carefully, but it didn't keep her from being nervous. Her hands vibrated against the steering wheel every time she noticed a police car. Charrise made sure to blend into traffic, extra careful to not call any unnecessary attention to herself. She had rented a black Toyota Corolla and maintained a speed no more than seven miles above the posted speed limit. She wore her seatbelt properly positioned over her left shoulder, and made sure to use her signal each time she switched lanes. Charrise used each and every rule of the road she'd learned in driver's ed.

Atlantic Station was Charrise's first stop. Hakeem had arranged for her to meet his cousin there to escort her through her first run. Before she could find a parking space she circled around the upper deck. There she noticed a man waving her down. He was wearing a grey hoodie, just like Hakeem said he'd be wearing. Charrise pulled up to the curb and rolled down the passenger side window.

"Andre?"

"Yeah Shorty, I'm Dre."

Charrise unlocked the door and Andre got into the car. What she saw next captivated her attention. Andre's chocolate brown skin was only the beginning to what Charrise could only describe as a fine ass man, simply put. He extended his hand to hers and she met it with a shake. His large hands totally covered hers as he sandwiched her hand between his. She couldn't take her eyes off him. Thick eyebrows, crisp white teeth, thick lips, piercing eyes, and he had the nerve to have long eyelashes to top it all off. Charrise allowed her hand to linger inside of his while she basked in the joy of this nice surprise. She had totally expected to see a similar version of Hakeem. Where were the dreads, or the gold teeth? He wasn't even wearing flashy clothes.

Breaking the awkward silence, Dre released her hands and said, "You ready to get this done?"

Andre led the way as Charrise navigated the car through Atlanta. As she drove, she regretted her purposeful plain Jane style. She wore her hair straight hanging at her shoulders, small diamond studded earrings, a long sleeved brown shirt, jeans and brown UGG boots. All of her nerves about her first trip as a runner had been replaced with self-consciousness and curiosity. Andre didn't seem like much of a conversationalist. He hadn't said much of anything outside of his turn by turn directions. Neither had Charrise.

Once they arrived at their destination, Charrise made her phone call and expected to part ways with her escort. Instead, Andre grabbed her hand and led her into the mall. She smiled and looked him up and down.

"What's this all about?" she asked.

"We have to make it look real." He said matter of factly.

Just as her smile faded, Andre seemed to have caught the conversation bug.

"It's not a problem is it? I wouldn't want to be invading on another man's woman."

"You good." Charrise responded.

"Cool."

"Thanks for helping me out today."

"Not a problem. It's not everyday I get commissioned to accompany a beautiful lady around my city."

"Thanks."

"I'm used to seeing women around here wearing a ton of make up, fake hair, and clothes that leave nothing to the imagination. Seems like you know it don't take all of that to get a man."

Unwilling to admit that she normally did look like the women he'd just described, Charrise went with the flow, smiling and nodding at his every word.

"So you already said you don't have a man. Is there anybody else you need to rush back to Charlotte to? Kids, friends with benefits?"

She laughed. "No and no."

"Aiight then how bout you let me show you a little more of my city. We can start with Gladys Knight's Chicken and Waffles."

"I'm down."

AS BRIANNA SAT on the couch eating ice cream, she glanced over at the three large garbage bags sitting it the middle of the floor. It was her third time looking at the bags. She was trying to mustard up the strength to start back counting all the money inside.

"Who would ever think a person would hate to see so much money," Brianna spoke aloud. Just as she was about to grab a handful to continue her count, her phone began to ring.

"Saved by the bell she thought," as she grab the phone and hit accept and speaker at the same time.

"What's up girl, what you up to?" Hakeem spoke loudly through the phone.

"Nothing, just over here hurting my hands trying to get this money counted."

"Hurting your hands? Please tell me you got some electronic counters in that bitch!"

"Electronic counters, hell no, I haven't even thought of that, I was over here doing this shit by hand!"

Hakeem burst out with laughter, "Girl you need to be saving those hands for me, not messing them up on that money. I got a couple of counters at my crib, how about you make us some lunch and I will swing by my place pick them up and come through and help you with your count."

"That's sounds good to me, what would I do without you Hakeem" Brianna responded in her daddy's little girl voice."

"I'm not thinking about what you would do without me, I'm more interested on what you would do with me!"

"Boy! Just go get the counters and we can finish this conversation when you get here."

With that, Brianna hung the phone up and went into the kitchen to make lunch. She pulled out some turkey burgers and Oreida French fries. As she placed both into the oven, she thought about how Tre used to love the weirdest things. Like stale cookies and his bread cold. He would open the cookie pack and leave it uncovered so the cookies would get stale quick. She remembered the day she asked him, "who puts bread in the refrigerator."

"Everyone in the hood, because if you don't the roaches will be in it real quick!"

Her thoughts were interrupted by the phone ring once again. She looked at the screen; it was her front gate, which meant Hakeem had arrived. She buzzed him up and went to take the food out of the oven. When Hakeem came through the door, he was dress in white form top to bottom. He had on a white polo fisherman's cap, a white wife beater, white shorts, and white polo shoes. For Hakeem it would not be complete without 30 Karats worth of Diamonds, hanging from his arm, neck, fingers, and ears. This was a part Brianna could live without. However her mind quickly moved, to the way his chest and arms bugled out of the wife beater. The three and half year bid had done his body good. You could see the eight pack through the tank top. When Hakeem hugged Brianna, she felt a warm sensation. His hands were so big and strong, that they touch when he wrapped them around her waist. She tried to deter the feelings to ask him to take her right then, by switching the mood to the dilemma at hand.

"So do you know how to work these things?"

"I wouldn't be the man I think I am if I couldn't," he said with a sly smile.

"Now where is your mind at? Because I know you not talking about the money machine's." Brianna said with a laugh.

"Shawtey I'm wherever you want me to be, but I know where I would like to be!"

"O yea where is that?"

"Eating my lunch!"

The answer had let Brianna down temporarily, "Well it's in the kitchen.

"No it's not," Hakeem interrupted. What I want for lunch is right here!"

He quickly pulled Brianna's small frame close to him. He was now sitting on the couch and her stomach was at eye level. He pulled up her shirt and began to kiss all over her stomach. Brianna began to run her hands through his thick locks. It felt so good that she didn't want him to move, until he began pulling her pants down. She didn't have on any underwear and could feel herself getting moist. Hakeem made his way down to her inner thigh, then to her clit. He was sucking and kissing with just the right amount of pressure. Her juices were overflowing, and then he stopped. Brianna glanced down at him with a strange look.

"Bri, turn around" he asked

As she turned around she stepped out of her pants.

Hakeem bent her over and started licking on her hole from the back. He went from her pussy to her ass. She had never felt this before, Tre was a freak but he had never ate her ass out. She began to rub on her clit while Hakeem was licking her ass clean. Brianna could feel the organism coming, her legs began to get weak, as her body was starting to shake. Hakeem spun her back around and put her legs on his massive shoulders.

"Shit," she thought, "I was about to cum!"

He stood up and began shucking on her clit again, her thighs became tighter and tighter around his neck. She could feel that organism coming back. She grabbed a fist full of locks, just in case he decided to stop again. She was starting to moan, then it became a scream!

"O shit, OOOO shiiiiiiiiiiiiiiiiit, don't stop, don't stop, I'm cumming, I'm cumming!" Her body became limp. Hakeem could feel the light wetness turn thicker in his mouth. He could also feel the loosening of her thighs. He knew she had came. He laid her on the couch. She still had her eyes closed.

Hakeem stood up over her, "Now where my other lunch at?" he asked like nothing had just happened.

"Wait and I will get it for you." Brianna said trying to steady her breath.

"Na shawtey you just relax, we got round two coming after a nigga get some food in him." He smiled and went into the kitchen.

Brianna checked out his backside as he strolled away. Damn she thought to herself, "I forgot how tired you feel after a good nut."

Brianna's phone rang, jolting her from her post-cum

thoughts. She looked down at the screen and saw that it was Lauren, her hair stylist. Brianna hit the accept button.

"Yes," she answered.

"Hey Bri how you doing girl? I wanted to confirm your appointment for this Friday and also tell you about our upcoming hair show." As Lauren went on and on about the upcoming show. Hakeem had shoved down the Turkey Burger and fries and was now ready for round two. He got down on his knees in front of her and held her legs stretched out as far as they could go. He began licking on her clit. Brianna was trying to keep her cool and half way listen to Lauren's conversation. But she could feel her pussy getting wet again.

"So Bri, can we look to put you down as a sponsor?"

"Huh," Brianna responded.

"For the hair show, girl are you listening to me?"

"Yea, yea that's cool." Brianna squeezed out.

"Ok so what level of sponsorship would you like?" By now Brianna was not even listening to Lauren. She had the phone in one hand and Hakeem's locks in the other.

"Look L just put me down for whatever, but I got to call you back!"

"Damn girl you running or something, because I—"

Brianna had hung the phone up and threw it to the opposite chair. Brianna's body started to tingle again, "Dang I know I'm not about to cum again this quick," she thought. There was something about Hakeem that turned her on, and she couldn't figure out why. Tre was the only man she'd ever been with, and she loved everything about making love to him. So much so that she'd never even considered being with anyone else. But for some reason she couldn't stop imagining how it would feel to have Hakeem inside her.

"Come on put it inside me" Brianna begged.

Hakeem stood up and looked at her with a sly grin.

He bent down and kissed her in the crease of her neck and shoulder. Then after placing one hand on each butt cheek he lifted her up, her legs straddling his body, and walked to Brianna's bedroom.

Hakeem was rough and aggressive in a way that Brianna had never experienced. He practically threw her on the bed and tore her clothes off. Once she was naked his callused hands swept over her shoulders, then breast, then torso, then continued to move down to her center.

Brianna looked over to her side table and saw a picture of herself with Tre.

Tears began to flood her eyes, but her body would not stop reacting to Hakeem's touch. Brianna remembered how tender Tre had been with her their first time. He had taken his time to romance her with candles and soft music. Brianna always knew that Tre and Hakeem were polar opposites, but she hadn't known until that moment that the differences were so wide spread. Tre's hands were soft to the touch and felt like silk when they glazed over her body. And when he tasted her, he took his time savoring every morsel. Hakeem ate her out like a man that hadn't had a meal in weeks. He licked fast and furious, brining Brianna to a peak before she could control it.

When Hakeem penetrated Brianna she felt like a new virgin. Her tight vaginal walls closed in around his dick squeezing it like she never wanted to let go. As his stroke pressed forward, her juices steadily increased leaving a shiny film on his manhood. Just as Brianna felt herself nearing yet another peak, Hakeem flipped her over and entered from behind. They matched each other's pace with thrust and pumps, over and over and over again, until they both came. Hakeem collapsed onto Brianna with his throbbing penis still inside her. Sweat dripped from his body onto hers as she panted trying to catch her breath.

Vibration from Hakeem's phone startled the pair from their trance. While Hakeem took his phone call, Brianna got into the shower.

With the door closed and the shower running, Brianna could hear bits and pieces of Hakeem's conversation.

"I told you... Stop being a bitch about it... Working..." he yelled.

Rather than letting his ranting dampen her mood, Brianna replayed their sexual encounter in her mind. Her nipples hardened just thinking about it. Brianna's lips curved upwards into a smile as she considered what round three would be like.

Chapter Nine

JUST LIKE OLD TIMES

One of Brianna's favorite places to go on sunny day was Freedom Park. She remembered going there as a little girl with her mom and sister. It had been her mom's only effort to give Brianna some relief from her stepdad. A mom and daughter's day out that occurred typically when things were too tense around the house. Brianna and Charrise always loved to play in the old train and walk around the lake to feed the geese. After Charrise moved in, they picked the tradition back up, leaving their mom out of the equation.

"I'm in love!" Charrise beamed to her sister as they walked around the man-made lake at Freedom Park.

Brianna rolled her eyes and shook her head, "Damn girl... In love? A handful of trips to Atlanta, and a couple rolls between the sheets and that nigga got you open already?"

"It's the same way Tre had you when ya'll first met."

"But I was a kid then. You're too old to be falling head first in love with some guy that you barely know."

Charrise couldn't stop smiling, "I know... but I can't help it. That nigga got me sprung and I ain't even ashamed to say it," she laughed.

Brianna couldn't help but to laugh with her sister, "We'll if you're happy, I'm happy for you. But now I wanna know when I get to meet him."

Charrise sucked her teeth, "I've been trying to get him up here, but for some reason he don't do Charlotte."

"I'm sure he'll make an exception for your big sister." Brianna insisted.

"I'll ask."

As the two made a second lap around, Charrise slowed her pace lagging a few steps behind her sister.

Brianna turned around continuing her pace backwards, "What's your problem now?" she asked.

"There's something I need to tell you… and I don't wanna see your face when I do."

"Oh God… that means it must be something bad."

"Well… just turn around and keep walkin!"

Brianna did as she was told and braced herself. Charrise had never liked to be the bearer of bad news. Brianna had taught Charrise this trick for saying things that she didn't want to have to stay a long time ago. In their household growing up, hurtful things went out of people's mouth daily. If he wasn't saying these things directly to Brianna, he'd send one of her younger siblings to do his dirty work. Brianna didn't like seeing her one true friend in the house turn on her, so they would stand back to back as Charrise would say things like 'Daddy said to tell you that I can't play with you anymore. He doesn't want his baby girl getting influnced by a bastard'. That way neither of them could see the tears in one another's eyes, and the sisterly bond they'd built wouldn't be broken.

Charrise blurted it out, "Mom's coming over."

Brianna reacted quickly, stopping dead in her tracks and turning her body.

"Coming over where?"

"To our house."

Brianna had rarely seen or heard from her mom since the

day she left the house. More often than not, she felt like an orphan.

"What the fuck Charrise? Why?"

"Cause she's our mom."

Brianna shook her head, "Correction. She's your mom. She stopped being my mom a long time ago."

That brought tears to Charrise's eyes. "Don't say that Brianna."

"Why is she coming over to MY house?"

"She's coming to OUR home because I invited her."

"And why would you do something like that?"

Charrise walked and sat down on a nearby hunter green park bench facing the lake. She motioned for Brianna to come sit with her. They sat in silence for a moment watching the ducks swim in the water.

"For starters, I'm giving her some money."

"Hmph," Brianna exhaled.

"And second of all, I just wanted to see her. Figured you might want to see her too. You must miss her… just maybe a little."

Brianna rolled her eyes and crossed her legs. That top leg rocked fast and steady like a pendulum.

Finally she said, "No, I don't miss her, but, she can come, on one condition. First you have to go somewhere with me."

Brianna clicked the button to lock the doors and initiate the alarm on her car door. She walked to the front of the car, linked arms with her sister and led her to the door. 85 South had brought them to Belmont, NC.

"You ready for this?" she asked.

Charrise simply nodded. Brianna opened the door to Shooter's Express and led her sister through. This was the same shooting range Tre had taken her to before gifting her the first gun she'd ever owned. He'd cautioned her that in his line of business, protection was a necessary evil.

Charrise jumped closer to her sister as she heard gunshots.

She looked over to see a large window revealing a line of shooters. At various paces the shooters loaded, pointed and then shot a variety of different guns at targets that looked like silhouettes of men.

A man behind the counter glanced at the girls giving them a once over. The pair looked out of place wearing stilettos, tight jeans and cleavage revealing shirts.

"Have you girls been her before?"

Brianna did the talking, "I have, but she hasn't."

"Ok, well… she'll need to take a look at the video."

Brianna pushed her sister towards the far end of the counter where there was a small TV/VCR combo. The TV played a short video about gun safety, as it ended the man behind the counter instructed Charrise to sign a waiver.

"Alright, now that that's done you can pick out your firearm, your ammunition, and your target."

Charrise looked at her sister, rolled her eyes and shook her head, "Is this really necessary?"

"Yes it is," Brianna said while she pushed her sister closer to the counter, "Go on… what kind of gun do you want?"

Charrise shrugged, "I don't know."

"Sir… what do you think is a good gun for my little sister to start with?"

The man looked at Charrise and looked at the case, then back to Charrise and back to the case, "Ummmm, I'd say a .22 would be a good place to start."

"Then a .22 it is… and one box of ammunition please."

The man pulled out one from behind the counter along with a box of bullets. Charrise's hands quivered as she picked up the cold, black gun and looked it over.

"And for you ma'am?" He asked.

"I have my own." Brianna pulled her .380 out of her holster, "I need ammunition for this though with two targets."

The girls took their things, and found an empty slot on the shooting range.

Charrise said, "I'm not sure it's such a good deal to be here shooting guns right before we have dinner with mama."

"I think it's the best idea yet," Brianna said while loading bullets into the .22. "Pay attention." She instructed her sister, "and go ahead and clip that target to the board."

"You're really serious."

"Yeah, I am. And you should be too."

"I just don't get how this fits into our lovely day. We we're at the park this morning, and after this we'll be going home to cook dinner together and ..."

Brianna interrupted her sister, "Let me stop you right now before you wreck my nerves. You need to learn how to protect yourself. We should have come here a long time ago. So just get with it. Plus, if you expect me to sit down and be cordial with your mother over dinner like we have a normal happy family... then I need to get a little aggression out. Is that ok with you?"

"Fine."

"Now relax... you just might enjoy yourself."

Both girls put on slightly tented shooting glasses along with silencer ear muffs. Brianna pressed her finger on the button moving the target about 15 feet down the line. She placed the revolver in Charrise's hands showing her how to hold it properly.

"Now aim and shoot."

Charrise pointed the gun towards the target and pulled the trigger. She was surprised at how good it felt.

"That was a nice first attempt," Brianna said, "but you aimed a little high. Hold your arms back out."

Charrise did as she was told. Brianna leveled Charrise's arms out, and tilted her hands straight.

"Now, look at the top of your gun. Focus your eyes. This time try to create a line from the tip of your gun to a place on the target."

Charrise pulled the trigger again. She pulled it for a third time, and again and again until there were no bullets left in the gun.

Brianna, pressed the button to bring the target towards them. Bullet holes were scattered around the sheet of paper, only a couple that had actually landed within the silhouette.

"Ok, you could stand to practice a little more. But for now, let your big sis show you how it's done."

She changed out the target, and eased it thirty feet away. Brianna placed her feet shoulder width apart, pointed and aimed her gun with sniper like precision. Boom, boom, boom, boom. As soon as she emptied her gun, she loaded in more bullets until they were all gone. When Brianna pulled the target back for review, all bullet holes were focused on the head and torso. Charrise was impressed and a little scared at how meticulous her sister had been. It made her eager to finish off the rest of her bullets. She pushed Brianna out of the way and started to load her bullets the way she'd seen it done. Brianna took the break to check her phone. Three missed calls. One from Hakeem, and two from an unknown number. She showed her sister.

"This is the real reason I wanted to bring you out her."

"Whatchu mean?"

"I've been getting all these phone calls from an unknown number. When I don't miss it, the person on the line doesn't say anything. Just sits there, breathing heavy."

Charrise looked at her sister with worry, "Who you think it is?"

She shrugged, "I don't know. Part of me thinks it's the dudes that hit Tre."

"For real?"

"Hell if I know. I just know that it's spookin' me, and we need to be prepared. Both of us. What I do know," Brianna picked up her target, "this is what they're gonna get if they come at me. We just gotta get you ready."

Chapter Ten

LOOK AT ME NOW

Lorraine walked into the home of her daughters and couldn't conceal her enthusiasm. As she looked around at the immaculately clean and lavishly furnished condo, she beamed with delight. Lorraine noticed Brianna on the far side of the room looking like a better version of the one she'd raised. She walked towards her first born with her arms outstretched, totally oblivious to the fact that Brianna did not share her excitement. Instead, Brianna noticed the grey hairs that her mother had neglected to dye and the extra pounds that seemed to bubble at her stomach. Brianna graciously accepted her mother's embrace.

Lorraine faced her daughter and said, "I'm proud of you. Looks like you've done well for yourself."

Brianna resisted the urge to roll her eyes. This was the kind of thing that most people longed to hear their parents say. But coming from Lorraine, it meant nothing to Brianna. Instead of addressing her mother's comment, Brianna plastered on a smile and changed the subject.

"We cooked all of your favorites."

"Oh really! That's my girls. I can't wait to eat it."

Brianna led her mother into the dining room where the

table was set. In the center of the table was fried okra, mashed potatoes, smothered turkey wings, corn bread and sweet tea.

The three women sat around the table rotating dishes as they each filled their plates.

In between bites Lorraine did her best to keep a conversation going, "So Bri your sister tells me you've got quite a lucrative business going." Brianna's eyes quickly dashed towards Charrise. "But she keeps leaving out what type of business it is. Tell me about it."

"Oh…um…" Brianna fumbled trying to think of a good lie to tell, "It's a retail venture… and um… distributing… you know… stuff like that."

Charrise jumped in, "Mama, we didn't invite you over her to talk to you about work. It's our day off."

"Ok, ok. I was just curious." Lorraine said as she loaded a second mound of mashed potatoes onto her plate, "We've really missed you around the house Bri. I really wish you'd come by more often."

Brianna laughed. But it wasn't a happy laugh. It was the kind of laugh that revealed disappointment.

"I know that things weren't always great at home. But we're family."

"It sure didn't feel like it," Brianna said.

"We'll I certainly did the best I could." Lorraine retorted.

Brianna was floored by this comment. "Excuse me?"

Charrise intervened as things started to get tense. She could see that both women had that special look in their eyes. That look could only mean one thing. It was as if the two were in a boxing ring. Both ready to defend their title, both willing to do what ever it took to knock the other down. And Charrise was the ref. She knew that this fight had to happen eventually. She was prepared to make sure they kept it clean, and didn't fight dirty. Charrise wouldn't stop them unless she had to.

"You know what Ma, I'm not going to sit here and say that you didn't do your best. It's obvious that you believe that you did. But I'm here to tell you, you're best just wasn't good enough."

"I see you're still too young and too naïve to understand what it means to keep your family together."

"Please," Brianna sucked her teeth, "The circumstances that I grew up in…. that cannot be considered family. I know people who treat their dogs better than I was treated. I never knew what it was like to have a real father. Shit, I never even knew what it meant to have a real mother… and that's your fault."

Lorraine's eyes widened, and her mouth dropped. "Brianna, how could you say that? I know things weren't perfect, but Lord knows I tried to protect you and show you love as much as I could."

"Yeah, as long as Herman wasn't looking. How do you think that made me feel? My own mama sneaking to show me love, while everyone else shared love freely around me."

"What else was I supposed to do?"

"I don't know," Brianna shrugged, "I guess the idea of taking your children out of that environment was too much to ask."

"Children?" Lorraine asked confused, "He was their father, I couldn't take them away from him. That wouldn't have been fair. They didn't have to go through what you went through."

"So it's ok to make one child suffer so the others can prosper?"

"It's called sacrifice. I made a sacrifice so my family could stay together and…"

Brianna shook her head, "No, I'm the one that made the sacrifice. And no one EVER asked me if I was ok with that. That's the type of sacrifice that a child should never have to make. But you know what, it's whatever Ma. We're not getting anywhere with this. I'm done with this conversation." She stood up from the table and walked away.

From the table Lorraine and Charrise could hear Brianna slamming her bedroom door.

Lorraine asked, "It wasn't that bad was it?"

"It was hard… on all of us in one way or another. The hardest for her."

"I didn't mean for it to happen like that."

"I know Mama," Charrise got up and took the seat next to her mother. She put her arms around her and said, "Brianna'll be alright. She's tough."

Tears started to pour from Lorraine's eyes. She nodded but didn't say a word.

Charrise pulled out a wad of cash and gave it to her mother. "Take this."

Without pause, Lorraine took the money and put it into her pocketbook. "I'ma go. You take care of your sister. And thanks for the help. I love you. Tell your sister I love her too."

Chapter Eleven

HERE I AM

Brianna straddled Hakeem sliding herself onto his firm erection. She grinded her center against his center at a steady pace. Back and forth. Side to side. Back and forth. Side to side.

"Ummmm," she moaned, "This is just what I need."

Then pressing her hands firmly on his chest, she pumped her butt up and down, over and over again. As a tingling feeling enveloped her body she increased her speed.

"Damn baby," Hakeem's face contorted and his eyes rolled back. He exhaled loudly before lifting her away from his erection. Hakeem flipped her over, pulling her ass to the sky. His rough hands rubbed Brianna from her shoulders down to her waist. He grabbed her on either sided, noticing that his thumbs almost touched in the middle of her back. As Hakeem pushed himself inside of her, his knees almost buckled beneath him. Brianna's insides were silky smooth. He moved in and out with ease. His force created a wavelike effect on her ass each time he entered her from behind. As Hakeem pressed his body forward, Brianna pushed back against him.

"Fuck me baby!" Brianna said, "Ooooooo. You feel so damn good... ooooooooooo."

Hakeem picked up his pace, fucking her hard and strong. Then pulled himself all the way out and flipped her again. With Brianna on her back, Hakeem teased her with the tip of his penis. He sucked one nipple, then the other. Brianna's body twitched in pleasure.

"Gimme that dick baby." She circled his body with her legs pulling him back inside of her. Hakeem did as he was told and pushed his dick deep.

"You like that?" he asked between short breaths.

"Ooooo yeah, give it to me."

Hakeem dug deeper and deeper inside of Brianna's warmth.

"Oh shit," he yelled, "I'm bouta cum."

Brianna grinded as Hakeem pumped. She felt the pressure rising up within her, bringing her to the point of climax with him. Hakeem rolled himself off Brianna and onto the bed. Simultaneously the duo panted as their chests rose and fell. Neither of them moved, or said anything.

Brianna woke up in the middle of the night to her phone ringing. She looked beside her and saw Hakeem asleep, his mouth wide open and he had no clothes on. She was naked too. She crawled across her bed and reached for her phone off the night stand. The caller ID displayed UNKNOWN. Brianna rolled her eyes and pressed talk.

"Hello."

The person on the other line didn't say anything.

"Quit callin my fuckin phone if you're not even going to say anything!" she said and pressed end. No sooner than she put the phone down it rang again. UNKNOWN.

"This shit is getting real irritating," Brianna said into the receiver.

"Hey Bitch! I'm outside."

"What?"

"I'm outside Bitch!"

Brianna kicked Hakeem awake, "Who the fuck is this anyway?"

Hakeem woke up startled and groggy. He stood up and stumbled to the bathroom.

"Why don't you come out here and see…. Bitch!" Yelled a high pitched, nasally voice.

"I ain't gone be too many more bitches." Brianna fired back.

"Oh you a bitch alright! You must be fuckin my man. Got him over here spending the night… you got some mutha fuckin nerve. You need to come down here to get your ass kicked before I throw a brick in this flyy shit you got down here."

"What the fuck!" Brianna ran to the window and saw a short chocolate brown girl with blonde highlights in her hair, standing in the middle of the parking lot. Brianna hung up the phone and started putting on her clothes immediately.

"Hakeem!" she yelled.

Hakeem rushed out the bathroom, "What up?"

"Yo bitch down stairs talkin bout she gone fuck up my car."

Just then, Hakeem noticed that Brianna was getting dressed. He quickly put on his clothes too. They rushed down stairs and into the parking lot.

The short brown girl was still standing over her car. Tears were streaming down her face and she clenched a brick in her right hand.

"Tiff!" Hakeem yelled, "What the fuck are you doing here?"

"I knew you were fuckin this bitch!"

Hakeem walked up to her and snatched the brick out of her hand. He flung it to the side and pulled her towards her car.

"Y'all shady as fuck!" She yelled back to Brianna, "How you gone fuck your dead boyfriend's best friend?"

"Go inside Brianna," Hakeem said. "I'll handle this."

Brianna was speechless. With nothing to say, she turned around and went back inside. She lay across her bed, guilt seeping into her brain. Tiffany's last words kept repeating in her mind. *How you gone fuck your dead boyfriend's best friend?* Brianna had to admit it to herself, it was shady. She didn't mean for it to happen like that but it had. It was convenient... and besides that, it just felt so damn good.

Thirty minutes later, Hakeem came back inside.

"My bad," were the first words that left his lips. "That was my baby mama. She trippin'. We ain't even toge—"

Brianna shook her head and stopped him, "No need to apologize... or even to explain."

Hakeem nodded, "Look, I gotta get outta here. You know I'm on probation and I don't need another charge. I have to meet with my probation officer this morning. They probably gone do a piss test. Shit, I just need to swing by the house and get prepared."

"Aiight," Brianna responded. "Just don't forget my sister's birthday is this weekend. We all goin out. Ya boy from ATL even comin up."

"Oh yeah?" Hakeem responded, "He comin' to Charlotte?"

"Yeah, be here Friday."

"Damn I didn't think my nig even did Charlotte like that, but ok. I'll holla at you later."

Chapter Twelve

A NIGHT ON THE TOWN

Brianna looked in the mirror and was satisfied with her appearance. She wore a grey, lavender and white color blocked mini dress from Bebe, paired with grey peep toed stiletto hills. The dress's sweetheart neckline showcased her small but perky breast, while the spandex material highlighted her ample behind and small waistline. She smoothed down her hair; it was parted in the center with long thick curls. After touching up her mascara and glossing her lips Brianna looked at her watch. It was 10:00pm. She had just enough time to meet her sister at the suite she was staying in downtown before heading to the club.

Charrise had put to use some of her nastiest bedroom techniques to convince Dre to come to her Birthday party in Charlotte. But he only agreed on one condition. That she would allow him to get them a suite during his stay in town. It would be part of her birthday gift, and Dre said he just didn't like staying in other people's houses. Charrise agreed, thinking his request wasn't too much to ask.

At a quarter after 10, there was a knock on the suite door. Charrise opened the door to her sister holding a small Tiffany blue box with a white bow.

"I come bearing a gift," Brianna announced with a smile.

"Oooooh," Charrise cooed, "I wonder what it can be."

Charrise opened the door wide and let her sister in. Brianna walked into the suite scanning the room for her little sister's beau. He was nowhere in sight.

"Happy Birthday Sis," Brianna said while handing over the box."

Charrise took a seat at the table and pulled one side of the tied ribbon until it fell loose. She opened the box to reveal a necklace with three overlapping charms. An open heart pendant, a tiny lock charm with a C and a four leaf clover.

"Thank you," Charrise said as she wrapped her arms around her sister's neck.

Over Charrise's shoulder Brianna saw Dre for the first time. He stood towering in the doorway of the suite's bedroom. He was stone-faced as he met her glance. Brianna was a little startled by the coldness of his first impression.

"Babe," his deep voice demanded a quick reaction from Charrise.

She turned and smile, "Oh hey. My sister just got here, come over here to meet her."

Dre walked over to the girls and forced a smile on his face. He extended his hand towards Brianna, "Hey."

Brianna stood, pushing his hand away; instead embracing him in a hug, "Nice to finally meet you." She stood back and gave him a once over, before looking back to her sister, "You did good Lil' sis… he's handsome."

Charrise laughed, and Dre did too. It seemed like he was starting to loosen up a bit.

"Now just make sure you take good care of my baby sis." Brianna said. "You look good Charrise."

"You think so?" Charrise twirled and rolled her eyes all at the same time, "Dre seems too think it's too much." Charrise wore a black banded dress with cap sleeves that hugged her every curve. There was a cutout in the back hovering between her shoulder blades and her ass.

Brianna shook her head, "No, I think it's cute. Now let's get up out here, you know Luna be pack on Sunday's and Fresh and Ree both owe me bottles."

As they drove threw downtown Charlotte Brianna, couldn't help but be a little bothered by the fact Dre had insisted they take separate cars. Hell, Luna was only a couple of blocks away and it was hard enough getting one parking space, let alone two. When they pulled up to the club Brianna saw a familiar face out front.

"Hey Bay, I know you saved a space for me and my peeps," Brianna spoke in her school girl voice.

Bay was the head of security and even though his job was to be an asshole. He had a soft spot for beautiful women.

"Bri babe you know I got you and whoever rolling with you, just next time tell your fine ass sista, don't be bringing no nigga with her!" Brianna laughed and handed him a $50.00 dollar bill. Once they were inside, Fresh escorted them to their VIP table where Ree and Pop were already seated with bottles of Cirico and Patron everywhere. As they approached their VIP section, they heard No Limit Larry over the microphone.

"I see Brianna and Charrise in tha building!"

The girls beamed as they walked through the crowd with everyone in the crowd looking at them.

No Limit Larry continued, "I wanna give a special shout out to Baby Girl Charrise cause today's her B-Day! We have a little birthday surprise for her."

Sunshine Anderson stepped up to the stage and pointed at Charrise, "This is from me to you." The DJ cut the music and Sunshine's voice filled the building with a melodic and soulful rendition of Happy Birthday. Charrise couldn't stop smiling.

The table in the VIP area was already stocked with bottles.

"You really trying to get a bitch drunk?" Charrise shouted.

Everyone was having a goodtime, except Dre. He had taken a seat on the other end of the couch. Every time Charrise would hug a guy, the grimace on his face would get angrier. Brianna spotted him over in the corner and went to try to create conversation.

"Dre why you over here by yourself, you don't want anything to drink."

"Nah, I don't want to drink anything from them niggas, if I want something I can buy it myself!"

"Wow, it's not like that, we all peeps and we show love like that to each other, it's a Queen City thing." Brianna said while laying her hand on his shoulder.

"Nah fuck that, your sister over there straight playing me, talking with them other niggas. I didn't come up here for this shit!"

"Dre, you really tripping. They just wishing her a happy birthday, and that's it."

"Bri, trust me, I know that nigga KB, he used to live in the A, and I know how he get down. And if them niggas hanging with him I know how they must get down. That nigga don't be having no bitch around him he ain't trying to fuck or didn't already fuck!"

"Little bro you really got my sista twisted, she not one of them type of women. Plus she really likes and cares about you. Let me get her over here so y'all can get this shit cleared up."

Brianna walked over to Charrise and let her know that her man was over there acting like a real bitch. "Girl that nigga's must be drunk or something, Is he always this jealous?" He over there tripping because you over here talking to KB.

"Who ya'll talking about?" KB asked.

Brianna and Charrise looked in Dre's direction.

"O nah, that's my nigga Dre, you fucking with him?" Charrise nodded her head yes. "Let me go let this nigga know we family."

As KB went over to talk to Dre, Brianna and Charrise followed.

"Yo what up bro?" KB extended his hand.

"Man get your hand out my face!" Dre responded with anger.

"Dre, bro it ain't like that, this family."

"Man, fuck that get out my face nigga!"

"Yo bro, I'm trying to let you know what's up, but I ain't going be too many more niggas!"

Dre stood up and squared off on him. Charrise grabbed Dre and Brianna stood in front of KB.

"Bro, it's all good, please go get a drink for me," Brianna said trying to defuse the situation. Charrise had pulled Dre to the side and Brianna could see they were engaged in a heated discussion. Finally, Charrise came over.

"Bri, he a little drunk that's all, and he really just wanted it to be me and him for my birthday, so we going to go on back to the hotel, ok?"

Brianna shot her a yeah right look. "You know we're going to talk about this tomorrow, right?"

"Yea I already know sis, but everything cool, trust me."

"It ain't you I don't trust. Call me later," Brianna said while looking at Dre with the evil eye.

"I guess it was good we drove separate cars!" Charrise said with a half-smile.

BRIANNA SAT STRAIGHT UP in bed startled by her ringing phone. She had just got to sleep good since getting home from the club. She recognized the familiar ringtone as the one she'd assigned to Charrise. She shook her head and laid back down. No way was she talking to a drunken Charrise about her jealous boyfriend in the middle of the night. But the phone just kept ringing and ringing. Finally Brianna answered the phone with attitude coating her voice.

"What!" she yelled.

At first all she could hear were sniffles, and then she heard Charrise say, "I need you to come get me."

"Huh?" Brianna asked.

"Come get me… please."

"Ok, ok…. Where are you? Where's Dre? Did something happen?"

"I'm in the bathroom of the hotel lobby. Just come now… call back when you get here."

Brianna hurried to throw on some sweats and rushed to her car. She headed north on I-77 speeding to merge onto I-277 to get to the heart of downtown Charlotte. She picked up her cell phone and dialed her sister's number.

"I'm outside."

When Charrise got into the car Brianna said, "What the fuck happened to you?"

The entire left side of Charrise's face was swollen and bruised. Tears began to flood from Charrise's eyes.

"Just drive."

Brianna switched gears and headed back towards the highway.

"Did Dre do this?"

Charrise only nodded.

"Oh my god!" Brianna's anger started to rise, "He's crazy if he thinks he's gone get away with putting his hands on you!"

"Just take me home, Bri."

"Fuck that! That nigga gone find out what it means tonight to put his hands on you! I'ma take you home, but this shit ain't over."

At the condo the first person Brianna called was Hakeem.

"Sup," he answered on the first ring.

"What's up is that ya boy put his hands on my sister."

Hakeem said nothing.

Brianna looked at the phone. The call was still connected. "You heard me? She asked.

"Yeah, but what you expect me to do about it."

"Something!" she yelled.

"Calm down now," Hakeem said, "I can't get involved in that. That's their business, and you need to stay out of it too."

"What the fuck you mean stay out of it? That ain't gone happen. This big ass mutha fucka got her face all bruised up... that ain't a fair fight... and if he don't wanna fight fair, I got something for his ass!"

"Aiight shorty... you need to calm down for real. Yo sister with you?"

"Yeah, in her room now."

"Then just chill... she ain't dead... it'll be aiight."

Brianna shook her head and pressed end on the phone. She couldn't believe her ears. As long as she had anything to do with it, Dre was going to get a taste of his own medicine. Brianna scrolled though her phone until she came to the name Kasy. Kasy was a guy from Queens who Tre would call when he had situation's that needed to be dealt with. There were a couple of times some people had jumped the fence on money owed. Kasy seemed to always have the conversation needed to get them back with full payment in hand. Since it was obvious Hakeem wasn't going to handle it, she knew she had to call someone she was familiar with.

Kasy picked up on the first ring "This Kasy."

"Hey Kasy this Brianna, Tre's Wife."

"O hey Bri, my condolences on your lost, sorry I wasn't able to make it to the funeral, I was away on some business, but how you doing?"

"Well not so good, which is my reason for calling you." Brianna gave Kasy a full rundown of what had gone down, they agreed on a fair amount for compensation. She let him know she didn't want to kill Dre, just let him know not to put his hands on her sister anymore. And to make sure he never contacted Charrise again.

"Don't worry Bri, I will make sure he get the message loud and clear." Kasy assured her.

"Well just make sure you give me a call when you have him, I want to see him when you finished. It's important that he know I did this to him!"

"I got you, Ma, I'll hit you later. One."

Brianna hung the phone up and went to check on Charrise. She was still fast asleep. The Oxycontin Brianna had given her had her out cold. Good, she thought to herself. Brianna knew Charrise didn't have the heart to be a part of what was about to go down. Shit, until a couple of months ago she wouldn't have been able to. Tre had all ways told her that this life changes you, you can never change it! Those words rung heavy in her head now. She had to let Dre know he had violated on two levels. First that was her sister, but Brianna was also the boss. She knew that had she been a male, there was no way a man would have beaten Charrise like that. He would have known the consequences.

It was late the next day when Brianna received the called from Kasy with instructions on where to go. She had to drive about 45 minutes outside of Charlotte to Gastonia, NC where Kasy and his crew had Dre held up at.

When she pulled up, she gave him a call on her cell phone, "Hey I'm outside."

"Ok, pull into the garage."

After she got out the car, Kasy escorted her to the upstairs bedroom where Dre's body was duct taped to a chair. His arms were out stretch across a small table, with his hands hanging off the ends. Brianna looked over at one of Kasy's henchmen.

"Well since he likes to put his hands on women, we figured if we break them, he would remember next time to keep them to himself."

Dre's head was down, but she could see blood dripping out of his mouth. Brianna grabbed his head and lifted it up. She wanted him to see her and know she had done this to him.

"Now the next time... she paused, no it won't be a next time. But if you ever call my sister or even think about touching her, I want you to remember what this feel like!" She grabbed his hand to bend it back, but something caught her eye. She looked again, was her mind playing tricks on her?

"Somebody cut on the lights" Brianna yelled.

"What's wrong Bri?" Kasy asked. "This is the right nigga isn't it?"

"Cut on the damn lights I said!" Brianna yelled even louder.

When the lights came on Brianna had a chance to examine his hands extremely well. Her eyes had not failed her and she had indeed saw exactly what she thought. There was the tattoo with the word "Smalls" exactly where she remembered. This was the same nigga that shot her that night.

"Bri, you ok?" Kasy asked for the third time.

Brianna looked at him, "Yea everything ok, but we need to renegotiate, he not leaving out of here tonight alive. Let me hold your gun."

"Remember this?" Brianna stood beside Dre with the gun pointed at his temple. Dre could feel the tip of the gun against his head. He didn't speak. He closed his eyes, breathing short and panicked. He was stuck in the chair. There wasn't a damn thing he could do.

"You should. This was the same way you stood over Tre when you came into our home," Brianna's voice got louder with every word she said, "and murdered him!"

Even with rage filling every inch of her being, Brianna couldn't bring herself to pull the trigger. But she wanted to. Wanted him to die like Tre had died, but first she had to know who his partners were. She wanted revenge on, not one, but all of the men that were responsible for turning her life upside down.

Brianna took the gun and placed it at Dre's chin pushing his face towards her own. He avoided eye contact at all cost, stretching his gaze in the opposite direction.

"Who were your partners?" Brianna asked simply.

Dre's silence only angered Brianna more. She took the gun and jabbed it into his crotch. He jumped, looked at her with pleading eyes.

"Ok, now that I have your attention… answer my Goddamn question!"

"I… I….. can't say," he murmured.

"So, you're telling me that keeping this secret is worth getting your dick blown off?" Brianna pressed the gun deeper into his groin.

He jumped again, "No!"

"Then tell me."

Before Dre could say anything, his phone rang. Brianna took a moment to dig it out of his pocket. It was Hakeem. She hadn't spoke with him since the disappointing phone call when he took the hands-off approach to her sister getting roughed up. But now he was calling Dre. She was losing all respect for him.

"I think I'll keep this." Brianna said putting the phone in her own back pocket.

Dre started to make a mental note of his surroundings. But as he looked around, despair seemed to overcome him. He started to remember more about the night. The men coming to get him, and the first few blows before he fell unconscious. He could see silhouettes of men a few feet behind Brianna. They were not alone, and he knew that he could not escape.

"It wouldn't even matter if I told you now. He's in the pen…"

Brianna paced back and forth in front of Dre. She knew that she wasn't going to get the truth out of him. Even if he did provide a name, there was no way for her to verify if it was even true. For all she knew he'd give her a fake name. As much as she wished she was in that moment, she wasn't a murderer. She wasn't going to kill him. But she knew who would.

"Kasy rock this nigga to sleep for good!"

"It would be my pleasure Bri." Kasy grabbed the gun from Brianna, stuck it to Dre's head and pulled the trigger.

AT HOME, Brianna placed the cell phone on the table and stared at it. By the looks of things, this was a man who never checked his voice messages. She figured that catching at least one of Tre's murderers was certainly better than none. But that didn't mean she wouldn't keep looking for the others. To start she was going to go through Andre's phone. Maybe, she thought, she would remember his voice if she heard it on the voice mail. If not that, then at least she could find out who was in his inner circle and go from there. She knew that it was farfetched to think that she'd get any information from old voice mail messages, but it was at least worth a try. Brianna's eyes were heavy with exhaustion. She picked up the phone and headed down the hall. First, she checked in on her sister. Charrise was still sleeping like bear in hibernation. Snoring too. In her bedroom, Brianna turned Dre's cell phone off and tucked it safely away in her night stand. She undressed to her panties and eased underneath her duvet. It didn't take long her body to relax. She got cozy in the center of her bed and fell asleep.

The next day Brianna woke up to the smell of sizzling bacon. She looked over at the alarm clock. It was 1:00pm in the afternoon. Charrise was in the kitchen cooking a big breakfast and trying to act normal. When Brianna walked in she was stirring cheese into a pot of grits.

"You hungry?"

"Yup… and it smells good in here."

Charrise turned to her sister and smiled. Brianna winced at the, now darker, bruises that on the side of her face. She shook her head, "Are you alright?"

"I'll be fine."

"I'm sorry. If it wasn't for me… you would have never met that jerk."

"Don't… it's not your fault. He's the asshole."

"Well, you don't have to worry about him anymore."

"What…" Charrise asked.

Brianna interrupted, "Let's just say it was a loooong night. And," she pause, "as it turns out… he was one of the guys that came here that night Tre was murdered."

Charrise's mouth dropped open, "Are you sure."

Brianna nodded. "Positive."

"Damn Bri… that's fucked up. How'd you find out."

Brianna told her sister about the tattoo. She filled her in on everything that happened that night. She even told her about the phone. Charrise didn't want to hear any of the messages. What she'd learned about the guy that she, only a day ago, thought she was in love with was more than enough. She wanted nothing more than to get over him.

After breakfast Brianna sat back at the table staring at the phone. She turned it on and noticed that there had been half a dozen missed calls from Hakeem. Funny, she thought, because he still hadn't called her. Brianna pressed the green button on the phone and, scrolled down to the option to play voice mails.

"You have and twenty three new messages," the phone said.

"Damn," Brianna said out loud. What kind of crazy voice mail service kept that many messages saved.

The first message had been left only a few weeks ago, "Hey babe," a female voice said, "it's me. I wanna see you tonight… I got something special for ya…" Brianna pressed seven to delete the message. That female voice was not her sisters. She couldn't believe that Dre had the nerve to put his hands on her sister, when he clearly had another woman on deck. Various female voices flooded Dre's voicemail. It was obvious to Brianna that Dre had a roster about as long as an NFL team. She shook her head. Niggas. Nearly every message had been from a woman.

Half way through, Dre's phone rang. It was another call from Hakeem. Brianna didn't answer, allowing the call to roll over to voice mail. Next her phone vibrated against the dining room table. It was Hakeem calling her phone.

"Hey," Brianna answered dryly.

"Sup, I was just checkin on you."

"Ummm hmmm," she responded.

"So, how'd everything turn out last night?"

"Fine."

"Did Dre and Charrise work it out… or what?"

"Nothing to be worked out," Brianna kept it short. After Hakeem had blown her off the other night, she wasn't really feeling him.

"Look, I'm sorry I couldn't help the other night. You just kinda put me in an awkward spot. I didn't want to get in the middle of that… You know?"

"It's cool, it was handled."

"What… you talked to him?"

"You already said you didn't want to get in the middle of it, and I'm not in the mood to talk about it. Let's just drop it ok."

"Aiight."

"I'll talk to you later though. I'm in the middle of something." Brianna wasn't quite ready to get Hakeem mixed up in this. He had been Tre's best friend, and she didn't even want to think about what he would do if he found out that Dre had something to do with the murder.

It took Brianna hours to get through the messages, and just as she was ready to give up, a familiar voice spoke on the voice mail.

"My nig," Hakeem said, "Just wanted to give you a heads up. Bri just called me trippin' cause you hit her sister or something. Try to steer clear of her, aiight."

The next message was from Hakeem as well.

"I haven't heard back from you. Call me back. We need to be careful about all this."

WE. The word confused Brianna and piqued her interested all at the same time. Hakeem hadn't been a part of Dre hitting Charrise, so what the hell was he talking about? That was the final voicemail, so she hung the phone up.

Charrise looked at her, "Did you find anything?"

"Not what I was looking for, just a bunch of voicemails from hoodrats." She and Charrise began to laugh.

"Shit I could imagine what the text messages look like!"

Brianna looked at Charrise like she had just solved the jeopardy final question.

"Damn girl, I didn't even think about that!" Brianna began to scroll through his texts. If she thought he had a bunch of voicemails, she wasn't sure what you would call all these damn texts. Then she saw a name and number that was familiar. It was Hakeem's. she clicked on the text so she could view the whole chat, then scrolled to the top.

YO WHAT UP KID, OL' *girl trying to get me to come up your way for her b-day*
Yeah, her sister told me, shit come on up my nigga
You know I said I wasn't come back there after that work we put in
Man, fuck that. Come on up here, it's all good
You sure it's cool?

Man, I'm fucking the bitch you didn't kill that night!
Word?
Yeah, my nigga, I got to thank you for fucking that shit up. She got some good pussy and the bitch is the plug
Damn nigga you a fool! Fuck it then I will see you this weekend!
Brianna couldn't even continue to read the rest. The truth was right there in her face. It hit her like an 18-wheeler going 80 miles an hour straight on. Brianna got a sinking feeling in the pit of her belly. Her eyes glossed over as she thought about the night she was shot and Tre was killed. She shook her head no. There had to have been another way. She tried to convince herself that she was misunderstanding the messages. Not only had she fucked her man's best friend, but also his killer. How had she been so stupid? The words Hakeem's baby momma shouted on that day began to ring even louder in her head. If Hakeem thought he was going to get away with this, he had another thing coming, Brianna thought to herself.

THE NEXT MORNING Brianna lay in her bed staring at the ceiling. She was the one who needed the sleep aid that night. She had tossed and turned all night. She knew Tre was looking down on her shaking his head. How had she violated him like that for some temporary pleasure? Forget that right now, she thought to herself.

"Babe how we going to get this nigga back?" Brianna shouted towards the ceiling. She knew that a quick death would be too good for Hakeem. He had to suffer a long slow death, but how? She continued to think. Brianna had thought about calling Kasy, but changed her mind knowing that he and Hakeem had to have had a relationship. She figured that he might even tip Hakeem off to her plan and she end up in the crisscross. Shit, Kasy was a hired gun, he would go with whoever he thought would benefit him the most. She knew that she had to handle this on her own.

"Tre please let me know what to do," she screamed again. Suddenly a big smile came across her face. Just that quick, Tre had answered her request. She knew what she had to do and exactly how to do it.

"Charrise!" Brianna yelled loudly. "Charrise, Charrise!" Charrise came running into Brianna's room.

"What is it sis, is something wrong?" Charrise asked, trying to catch her breath.

"I got it, we about to get this nigga, just me and you."

"Huh?" Charrise asked confused.

Brianna ran the whole plan down to Charrise. It took two hours of back in forth strategizing before both girls were satisfied that the plan was perfect. Hakeem would not know what hit him, and he would always remember the Campbell sisters. This, they were sure of.

BRIANNA TOOK a deep breath and hit send on her phone.

Hakeem picked up on the second ring, "Yo what's up, shawtey? I'm glad you hit a nigga, because I don't want what's going on between my man and your sista, to fuck up what we got going on. I got real love for you shawtey and...."

"It's all good Hakeem, let's just move on," Brianna spoke cutting Hakeem off. It was all she could do just to speak to him. There was no way she was going to hear this love shit from him. Love was something she knew was lost when she buried Tre.

"Yea you right shawtey, let's just move on." Hakeem agreed with her statement.

"Well, beyond that, the reason I was calling you was because that work is coming in tomorrow morning and I want to make sure everything is still a go?"

"Hell yea, ain't nothing change, we got to get this bread babe."

"Well I have twenty plates laid to the side for you, so you can pick them up tomorrow after 1pm; you still have the code to the storage right?" Brianna asked.

"Yea babe, I'm all good on that, but when can I see you? I got a hard on waiting on you." Hakeem spoke with a slight laugh.

Just a few days ago, Brianna would have loved to help Hakeem with his hard on. Now she wanted to throw up at the thought. But she knew she had to act like everything was normal.

Brianna put on her sexy voice and whispered, "Well you hold that hard on until tomorrow, and after you done with work, I'm going to put in some real work."

Hakeem smiled at the thought. "Ok, bet. I will see you tomorrow fo sure," Hakeem hung up the phone and looked into the rear view mirror at himself.

"Damn nigga you the man!"

The next morning, Hakeem rolled out the bed, he looked down at the stripper he had met last night at Club Onyx. He pulled the covers back to reveal her phat smooth ass. He thought about getting back in the bed and getting another sample of it, but then remembered he had to tighten Brianna up later. So he shook her leg.

"Shawtey get up, it's time to go." The thick light-skinned young woman eased slowly out the bed and began to get dressed. Once Hakeem had got her out to her car and gave her some breakfast and gas money, he went back in to get ready for his day. He threw on his so called work uniform, which consist of all black everything. That meant black tee, black jeans, black shoes, black fitted cap, and black Gucci shades. "I guess I will go low key and take the Honda Accord out," he thought to himself. When he got to the storage unit, he put in the code and the gates raised up. He looked at his phone to see what the storage room number was. Once he got to the matching number on the door. He grabbed the key to unlock the bolt. Inside he took a count of the drugs that were left for him. He counted again, to make sure he was correct. Indeed, it looked like Brianna made a mistake. He was counting 23 kilos, not the 20 he usually got.

Yeah, Brianna had fucked up and to his benefit, Hakeem thought. It was no way he was going to pull her coat to this error. She would have to learn this one the hard way. Hakeem threw everything into his trunk and proceeded to his next destination. Once he pulled up to the house in Charlotte's north side. He drove the car around to the back of the old broken down duplex. Hakeem's workers were waiting in the back to greet him. "Pull three of those out for me and put them in the back seat. A nigga got a little blessing today!"

"Y'all get all this shit broke down and I'll be back later to check in. Niggas, Onyx on me tonight!"

All the guys started cheering. They knew how Hakeem balled and they knew that night would be off the chain. He got back in the car just as his phone was ringing. He looked down and saw it was Brianna. *Damn, had she realized her mistake?* he thought. Either way it was no way he was going to admit to it, she was on her own. "Yo what's good babe?"

"Nothing, I was just making sure you were still coming by today."

"Hell yeah, I'm in route to you now." Hakeem responded

"Well hurry up I'm already wet just thinking about you. I want you naked before you step in my room."

"Damn, that's how you feel, shawtey? I'll be there in twenty"

"Well, I'm already in the bed waiting on you and I'm leaving the door unlocked."

Hakeem hung the phone up and pressed on the gas pedal harder. He made it to Brianna's house in what seemed like ten minutes. She buzzed him up and he was at the front door.

The door was slightly open and he pushed his way in. He started undressing on the way to Brianna's bedroom, as requested. By the time he reached her bedroom door, he was completely nude. He opened the door and saw Brianna laying on the bed face down. She was also naked and wet as promised. Hakeem immediately put his face in Brianna ass. He stared licking her ass and pussy from the rear. Brianna bit her lip, but not in ecstasy, his every touch was disgusting to her. She was on her stomach for a reason. She didn't want to have to look at him. It was bad enough she had to allow him to violate her like this, but she knew it was the only way her plan would work.

Hakeem raised his face up and began to rub his dick up against her pussy lips. They were wet to the touch. He began to enter her. Brianna gave him a fake moan. Hakeem began to take long, slow strokes.

Damn, I know how Whoopie felt in *The Color Purple*," Brianna thought to herself. She was trying to hold back the tears, while in her mind she kept asking Tre to forgive her. Finally, Hakeem began to cum, she could feel the fluid filling her box up. He laid on top of her, his body wet with sweat.

"Babe, let me up so I can take a shower." Brianna asked.

Hakeem rolled off her, glad that she didn't want seconds. He had already fucked the stripper twice last night and he didn't have another nut in him.

While Brianna was in the shower, she couldn't hold back the tears any longer. She wiped away tears and the water and dried herself off. By the time she came back into the bedroom, Hakeem was fully dressed.

"Hey shawtey, you know I got to get moving. I got to get this work off today so we can be ready to re-up next week, so I'll hit you later ok?"

"That's cool, just call me later," Brianna tried to muster a smile.

Once she was sure that Hakeem was gone, she quickly ran into Charrise's room. "Were you able to check the trunk?"

"Yes." Charrise responded

"Were the 3 kilos there?"

"Yep, right were you said they would be!"

"I knew that nigga would take the bait, this one time his greed is going to catch up with his black ass!"

"Did you call officer McFadden, like I told you?"

"Bri, I did everything like you said, trust me this nigga about to get his."

As Hakeem pulled out of Brianna's parking lot, he pulled out a blunt and began to fire it up. *Damn, Brianna got some good pussy,* he thought to himself. "A nigga need a good smoke after that."

He proceeded down Graham Street while hitting the search button on the steering wheel. He was trying to find his favorite song on his Gucci Mane mixed CD. He heard the sound first, then he looked up and into the rearview mirror. His eye's confirmed what his ears heard. All he could see was the blue flashing lights going off behind him. Damn he thought to himself, as he attempted to put out the blunt. Hakeem pulled the car to the side of the road. It started to look like half of CMPD was behind him. The African-American male cop walked up to his window. Hakeem had already grabbed his registration and license. He reached them to the officer.

"How you doing officer, did I do something wrong, I know I wasn't speeding?"

"Well sir you seemed to have been weaving back and forth through the lanes."

"Huh?" Hakeem asked, with a puzzled look on his face.

"Yes, and I can smell why. Please step out of the car, sir!"

Hakeem opened the door and the officer yelled back to the three officers standing at the back of the car.

"Can someone call a K9 unit?"

Hakeem started to get a sick feeling in his stomach. "There's no need for that sir, I just came from dropping my son off at my baby's momma house. I admit I lit up one up, here it is.

"There is nothing else in the car? Well do you give us permission to search the vehicle that will save us all some time. You know legally we can search it anyway, because the marijuana gives us probable cause."

Hakeem knew he had fucked up, but he wasn't going to help them. So he said, "Fuck that. Call the dogs, nigga."

"Ok, you want to play it that way. You guys cuff him and put him into the car."

Once the K9 unit pulled up it didn't take long for the dog to jump on Hakeem's trunk, like he had just saw a cat go into it. Hakeem saw the smile go across the face of the officer controlling the dog. He pulled the three Kilos of dope out and held it up. The entire group of officers looked back at Hakeem with smiles across their faces. All he could do was drop his head.

Chapter Thirteen

PAYBACK IS A BITCH

Brianna parallel parked her car on East Trade St., behind the Mecklenburg County Jail. Inside she pulled out her id and showed it to the guard. The officer passed her a key instructing her to put her valuables into a locker along the wall. Afterwards she walked through the metal detector with no issues. She pressed the button to the 7th floor. Brianna chose to sit at the last visiting window in the row. She waited for Hakeem to grace her with his presence.

Hakeem appeared behind the glass in a bright orange jumpsuit, his dreads neatly tied at the nape of his neck. He picked up the phone as he sat down in his seat. Brianna picked up hers as well.

"Man Bri, I can't believe I got caught up like this."

Brianna couldn't resist a smile, "It's crazy right?"

"Hell yeah," he shook his head, "this was my last strike. I go to court in a few weeks, but I can't really see a way out of this."

"What'd your lawyer say?"

"He said he'd try his best… see if he can find something… but I'm nervous."

Brianna's eyes went cold, "I guess this means Dre was right then, huh?"

"What'chu mean? Right about what?" Hakeem responded with a confused look on his face.

"That he should have never came back to Charlotte."

Hakeem shook his head, "I don't see what that has to do with anything."

Brianna sat back in her chair and crossed her legs, "You don't?"

Hakeem didn't respond right away. He sat there with a blank stare.

She shrugged. "It just seems to me that whenever he comes here… some shit goes down. Wouldn't you agree?"

Hakeem grimaced, "Where are you going with this, Bri?"

"It's like you said," she continued. "At least you got some good pussy out of all this…. I hope it was worth it."

Hakeem dropped the phone away from his face and looked at Brianna with wide eyes. Brianna stood up, placed the phone back onto the receiver, and walked away.

To Be Continued…

Keep Reading For A Small Excerpt From

Trapstar 2
"Trapping Aint Dead"

Trapstar Two Sneak Peek

TRAPPING AINT DEAD

The sky was blanketed in midnight blue as the black on black Ford F150 eased towards the house. Brianna sat in the passenger seat of Kacy's truck with her thighs on her hands attempting to hide the nervous energy that made them tremble. Brianna wasn't used to being on this side of the game. She'd felt at ease being behind the scene, doing all the things that kept her hands clean. But things had changed almost suddenly after Hakeem's arrest. Not only was there more money to be made, but there was definitely more money to be collected. There was no way should could afford to not collect on 20 kilos of dope. That was the one thing that she hadn't factored into the equation when she had plotted to set up Hakeem. While Brianna was satisfied that her revenge on him had been sufficient, she'd forgotten that he'd been somewhat of an ally when it came to her business. There was no time to sit around and mull over the details of this discrepancy. Instead she had to act, and she had to act fast.

Kacy looked over at her and asked, "You aiight?"

"I'm just ready to get this over with." Brianna said.

"Ok." He said as he eased around the corner and turned his headlights off. "I know Tre had to prepare you for this type of battle."

Brianna nodded, "He did... I just never thought I'd have to use it."

"Well... it's time to see what you're made of."

Kacy and Brianna got out of the car and walked to the door of the one story ranch house. They could hear a TV blaring from the porch, and saw lights on. Kacy stepped up to the door and slammed the side of his fist into the door three times. Almost immediatley the TV went silent, and the door cracked open. Kacy kicked the door the rest of the way open with his size 12 boots. Everyone inside began running. Kacy let off two shots into the wall. Everyone froze.

" All you niggas get on the couch". He motion with the 12 Gauge shot gun. As the four men sat on the couch. Breanna began to speak

"Look Muther fuckers, it seems to be some mis-under-standing on who to pay since hakeem is away. Well let me help you get this shit right. Who is Big D?" Istantly the other three men looked in the direction of the short heavey set man on the left end. Breanna walked up and stood in front of him.

"Put your hands on your knees nigga" Big D placed both his hands on his knees, and looked up at Breanna with a nervous look.

"Now Big D where is my money?

"Kesha already came and picked it up, Hakeem called me from the joint and told me to give it to her! Look I didn't know anything different so that's what I did."

"Nigga you gave that bitch my money?"

"Not all of it, there's $85,000.00 in the backroom"

Kacy moitioned to one of the other guys, to go to the backroom and get the money. He followed behind the man closely, until he pulled the money bag out the closet. When they enter back into the living room. He gave Breanna a heads up look. She was still standing over Big D.

Which hand you whip the dope up with?

"Huh?" Big D looked confused

"Which hand you cook with nigga, I don't want to put you out of work?" Big D still looked confused.

"Fuck it" Breanne placed the gun on top of his left hand and pulled the trigger!

"Got Damit!!! Big D hollerd

"Now nigga you will know the next time you hand my money to someone, that will be a hand you lose! She turned around and walked towards the door.

" O yea you nigga's be prepared, we got some work coming in next week. Anybody got a problem with working for me? All the men shook their heads no. Breanna turned and walked out the house.

Once her and Kacy got back in the truck, money and respect in tow.

Kacy smiled at Brianna, "I didn't know you had it in you."

Brianna laughed, "Like the saying goes... don't judge a book by it's cover."

Just as they made it out of the neighborhood, Brianna felt a familiar feeling bubbling up in her belly.

"Pull over."

"Now?" Kacy said confused.

"Now!"

As soon as Kacy stopped the car, Brianna slung the door open and vomit all over the pavement.

"Damn!" Kacy shouted.

Brianna wiped her mouth with the back of her hand and stumbled the couple steps back to the car.

Kacy sat there with a grin on his face, "I guess you're not as tough as we thought you were."

Brianna shook her head, "No, it's not that. I think I have a bug or something. Been throwing up like this for the last week or so."

Kacy's face went serious. He glared at Brianna like he could see right through her, first at her face, and then at her belly.

Available Now On Amazon Trapstar Book Two

About the Author

Blake Karrington is a Essence Magazine® #1 Bestselling novelist. More than an author, he's a storyteller who places his readers in action-filled moments. It's in these creative spaces that readers are allowed to get to know his complex characters as if they're really alive.

Most of Blake's titles are centered in the South, in urban settings, that are often overlooked by the mainstream. But through Blake's eyes, readers quickly learn that places like Charlotte, NC can be as gritty as they come. It's in these streets of this oft overlooked world where Blake portrays murderers and thieves alike as believable characters. Without judgment, he weaves humanizing back stories that serve up compelling reasons for why one might choose a life of crime.

Readers of his work, speak of the roller coaster ride of emotions that ensues from feeling anger at empathetic characters who always seem to do the wrong thing at the right time, to keep the story moving forward.

In terms of setting, Blake's stories introduce his readers to spaces they may or may not be used to - streetscapes with unkept, cracked sidewalks where poverty prevails, times are depressed and people are broke and desperate. In Blake storytelling space, morality is so curved that rooting for bad guys to get away with murder can sometimes seem like the right thing for the reader to do - even when it's not.

Readers who connect with Blake find him to be relatable. Likening him to a bad-boy gone good, they see a storyteller who writes as if he's lived in the world's he generously shares, readily conveying his message that humanity is everywhere, especially in the unlikely, mean streets of cities like Charlotte.

Made in the USA
Coppell, TX
24 October 2024

39129659R00066